GRACE BRENNAN

KISS THE GIRL

Formatting: Dark Water Covers & Formatting

CHAPTER 1

Payton Osmond quickened her steps as excitement flowed through her veins. It was finally the full moon cycle again and she was headed where she always seemed to be these days when she was able to walk around on two legs.

Her best friend Ailani Carter's house.

She was always happy to see her—spending her months locked in the lake was even lonelier now that Ailani lived on the surface—but her focus was on getting her hands on baby Ariel. She literally itched to hold her again.

Lani and Eric's baby girl was five months old now, with a mop of red curls and eyes a startling green, the shade a perfect blend of Ailani's moss green and Eric's pale green. She was smiling now, with a crease in her cheek just like her daddy's, and she was such a happy baby.

Payton couldn't love her more if she was her own—and it broke her heart that she missed out on so much while she was stuck in the stupid lake for the majority of the month. Ariel was growing like a weed, and already she was so different from the newborn Payton always visualized in her mind.

It wasn't like Payton had ever actually *enjoyed* being a

mermaid, cursed to live in Sapphire Lake and only able to walk on land three days a month—but nothing had ever made her resent it quite as much as this. She hated knowing she was missing so much of her honorary niece's life, and that Ariel didn't even know who she was, because she only saw her once a month.

It should light a fire under her ass to search even harder for her true mate, the man who could break the curse and allow her to live on the surface again. But for once in her life, she was barely searching for him.

It was strange—her clan was cursed a thousand years ago, and she'd never once *not* tried to find her mate. It was virtually impossible for hundreds and hundreds of years, since the lake was in the middle of nowhere with no one around. But once Aurora Falls—the town that sprung up next to the lake—came into existence, her hope had become strong again.

There wasn't a full moon cycle that had gone by since then that she hadn't been in town, praying each month that she'd meet her mate. She only got three days a month to search for him, and she hated giving even a single second of that time up, even for necessary needs like sleeping, eating or showering.

But the moment Ariel was born, the only thing she wanted to do during her time on land was spend every waking moment with the little angel baby. It was bittersweet, because she wanted nothing more than to find her mate and have children of her own—she wanted it with a sharp ache that stole her breath if she let herself become overwhelmed by the longing she felt.

But maybe spending so much time with Ailani, Eric, and Ariel was what she needed, though. Maybe she was searching too hard for her mate and it was time for a break. What was that saying? A watched pot never boils?

She finally broke through the tree line at their house, steps faltering and then coming to a stop when she saw the truck in the driveaway. Ugh. What was Gabe doing there? Narrowing her eyes, she debated for a long moment, wondering if she should just wait for him to leave before she went to the door.

Gabe was Eric's brother, and Payton was excited to meet him at first. Not because she thought they'd be potential mates—although, when she saw how gorgeous he was, she couldn't deny that the thought had popped into her head—but because she saw him as someone she could add to the very small list of family she had left.

After all, his brother was marrying the closest thing to a sister she had—and her own family died roughly a thousand years ago.

But it didn't take long after meeting him to realize he was a surly jerk who wasn't interested in new potential family members. Hell, he barely had time for the brother he had.

Guilt crept over her and she sighed before biting her lip. She knew what happened to him and she was a little ashamed of thinking badly of him. She knew intimately what tragedy felt like, but she had no idea what it felt like to lose a child. It wasn't fair of her to judge how he dealt that.

Everyone was different—just look at her and Ailani. They'd both been cursed by the witch to live as mermaids, and both lost every single person they knew back in their homeland.

Both basically lost everything.

But while Payton remained an eternal optimist, Ailani shut down after two hundred years. She pulled into herself, only ever interacting with her brother and Payton. Their coping methods were totally different.

Ailani had to shut down to protect herself, and she refused to search for a mate or even believe they were real. That was how she survived.

Payton had to keep her hope strong, and she searched unceasingly for her mate. That was how *she* survived.

And like she told Ailani months ago when her friend found Eric, there was no right or wrong there. They both did what they had to do to make it through the curse.

Maybe Gabe was just doing what he had to do to survive burying his child.

Didn't mean she had to approve, or even like the way he handled it. It was his choice, and if that was what he had to do to survive, who was she to judge? It wasn't like they were around each other very often, anyway. She'd only seen him three times since they met.

And, with that thought, maybe she'd just hang outside here for a little bit longer in the hopes that the number of times she'd seen him didn't have to change.

CHAPTER 2

GABE CARTER PUSHED HIS PLATE BACK, NEARLY groaning inside when he saw that Eric and Ailani weren't done eating yet. Little Ariel gurgled happily in her high-chair, and his eyes shot to her to make sure she was okay before he looked away just as quickly.

A sharp pain pierced his chest and he inhaled deeply, trying to push it down deep again. It was never far from the surface, but it was always right there hovering, just waiting on the opportunity to strike, when he was around his niece.

He never would have moved to Aurora Falls when Eric and Ailani got married and had a kid if he'd known how often they'd try to force him to come for dinner. But he hadn't been physically capable of being a three-hour drive away. There'd been too many thoughts bombarding him about all the things that could happen, all the ways tragedy could strike, and he had to be close by.

Hell, he still did, and he knew himself well enough to know he didn't regret moving close to them. He just wished seeing them—Ariel especially—didn't always feel like torture.

Would it be rude to leave before everyone was finished eating?

Probably. Dammit.

His eyes involuntarily went back to Ariel and he couldn't help the smile that twitched his lips up when he saw her grinning at him. Breathing deeply through the automatic renewal of pain burning through his chest, he felt the weird smile fade from his face.

Weird because he could count the times he'd smiled in the past three years on one hand with change left over. The stretch and pull of his lips felt alien and unnatural—a far cry from the man who'd always had a smile on his face and a joke on his lips.

That was what happened when a person's entire world imploded, though. Something like that would forever scar and change a person, and then one day, they wouldn't even recognize the reflection staring back at them in the mirror.

Fuck. He needed to think about something else before he lost it, right there at the dinner table with his brother and sister-in-law, while little Ariel looking on.

Shaking his head, he nearly snorted as faint amusement welled up inside him. He barely felt it, and it was no match for the pain lingering in his chest, but it was still nice to know he could feel it.

And he felt it every time he thought of his niece's name.

Only his damned brother could find a redheaded mermaid to fall in love with—and then have a daughter he named Ariel. It was all too much—his brother's name was Eric, one of his dog's name was Triton, and then he fell in love with a mermaid with red hair.

They even had a cat named Flounder now. Poor cat, named after a fish.

Gabe had been wary and mistrusting when his brother told him about Ailani—mostly because of how quickly he fell for her, how quickly he was throwing around words and phrases like *fate* and *meant to be*. Because Gabe had done the same thing once upon a time and ended up married to that bitch on heels formerly known as Julie.

But once he met Ailani, he had to admit, he really liked her. She was nothing like his ex, and he could see in an instant how much they loved each other. The puppy dog eyes they made at each other was a little sickening, honestly, but he was still happy for Eric. His brother deserved to have a happy and fulfilled life.

Still, when Eric sat him down and told him Ailani had been cursed by a witch a thousand years ago, forced to live in the lake as a mermaid and only able to walk on land for the cycle of the full moon, which was roughly three days a month...

He'd wanted to rush them straight to a psych ward and have them put directly into straight- jackets. Both of them. Do not pass go and do not collect two hundred dollars.

He was pissed as hell at Ailani for somehow managing to dupe his brother into believing something so ridiculous and pissed at Eric for actually believing it. Hell, pissed at *both* of them for believing it, because it'd been clear as day that she believed what she said, too.

Gabe's disbelief hadn't lasted long, though. They'd timed the big reveal just right, knowing he'd never in a million years believe it without proof. Apparently, once the curse was broken by Ailani finding her true mate, it worked in reverse, and for three days a month, she could turn into a mermaid again.

It was kinda hard to think they were batshit crazy when he was staring down at his soon to be sister-in-law, sitting in the lake with a very real tail.

And now even Ariel, his adorable, very much human-when-she-was-born niece, was the same as her mom. They'd dipped her in the lake when she was three months old, and now she could turn into a mermaid during the cycle of the full moon. It was all just too much for him.

On one hand, he was glad his brother thought highly enough of him to trust him with the truth. Hell, that he even wanted to tell him at all. But on the other, he wished they'd just kept that shit to themselves. He didn't need to know that the world he was living in wasn't the same one he'd known for thirty-two years.

Knowing that witches, curses, and mermaids were real did nothing to make him feel secure about the world he was living in.

"Gabe?"

Blinking at his name, he glanced up to find Eric and Ailani staring at him. Judging by how forceful his brother's voice had been, and the fact that they were both finished eating, he guessed they'd probably been trying to get his attention for a bit while he was lost in thought.

"Yeah, sorry. Woolgathering, I guess. Can I help you clean up?" he asked, willing them to say no so he could skip on out.

The universe must have been listening for once, because Ailani shook her head. "No, I got it. I hope dinner was more edible this time."

His lips quirked as he nodded. "It was great. That cooking class you two are taking is really paying off."

And if he still had the faint taste of burnt noodles in his mouth when he said that, well, his words still weren't a lie. The first couple of times he'd come over for dinner, he'd barely been able to keep from grimacing as he gagged, forcing the food down. Burned noodles were a huge step up from that mess.

Standing up, he quickly took his dishes to the kitchen

and rinsed them off, ready to get out of there before someone asked him to hold the baby again. He knew it hurt Ailani's feelings when he declined, and she was such a sweetheart. He didn't want to hurt her.

His heart just couldn't take holding a baby when he could never hold his own again.

Ailani and Eric both understood why. He knew that—but it still didn't stop them from asking. And lately, his brother had gotten a stubborn look in his eyes, like he was going to force the matter sooner rather than later. He wanted to put that off for as long as possible.

Walking back into the dining room, he stopped by where Ailani was holding Ariel, watching Gabe pick up the dirty plates. Reaching out, he slid his finger down his niece's satiny smooth cheek, his heart clenching painfully in his chest, before pressing a quick kiss to Ailani's cheek.

"Thanks for inviting me for dinner. I hate to eat and run, but I have a lot of work to do tonight."

She smiled up at him, her green eyes saying she knew he would take any excuse to split as fast as he could—just like he always did. "Thanks for coming. You're always welcome, you know that. Come over as often as you like."

Forcing a smile at the words she always said to him as he left, he nodded, raising his hand at Gabe and then quickly making his way to the door. He went outside, breathing a sigh of relief that quickly dissipated when his brother followed him out just as he was opening his truck door.

"Gabe, wait up."

Blowing out a breath, he forced the impatience he felt out of his expression, cocking an eyebrow as he watched Eric jog over to him. "What's up?"

"Listen, if you get a call from the house phone this

weekend, make sure you answer it, okay? Don't let it go to voicemail like you usually do."

Brow twitching, he studied his brother as he nodded slowly. "Why?"

Eric frowned. "You need a reason to actually answer the phone when I call?"

"No, not really, but I have a lot of work to do this weekend, and you know I don't answer the phone when I'm in the beginning stages of drawing new plans up."

"Like you *ever* answer your phone, working or not," Eric muttered under his breath as he rolled his eyes. "I know being an architect is a demanding career, but for someone who used to hound me about spending too much time at the veterinary clinic, you sure have changed your tune."

Gabe clenched his jaw to keep from replying that work was all that kept him sane these days, and his brother ought to damned well know that. "I'm still waiting for you to answer the question."

Eric narrowed his pale green eyes at him, and he could tell he was debating whether or not to keep hounding him about work, but in the end, he let it go. Thank fuck, because the last thing he wanted was to get into that with his hard-headed brother again. He just wanted to go home and wait in vain for the pain in his chest to ease once he was away from Ariel—not that it ever went away, but he still always hoped.

"Tai and Brandy asked Ailani and I to go on a trip to the city with them first thing in the morning. We won't be back until Sunday, and Payton's watching Ariel for us. We just want to make sure someone's nearby who can help if she needs it."

He frowned, uneasiness blossoming in his chest at the thought. He *couldn't* help with Ariel, not like that, because his heart couldn't take it—and he didn't *want* to be around Payton for any length of time.

She was cute, bubbly, hopefully optimistic—all the things he wasn't. All the things he couldn't handle being around.

And he refused to even *think* about the other reason why he didn't want to be around her.

"If you don't trust her to care for Ariel properly, why don't you—"

"What?" Eric interrupted, eyebrows high. "No, that's not it. We trust her one hundred percent. She loves Ariel like she was her own, and she's a natural with her. Our concern is if, Heaven forbid, something happens. She doesn't know how to drive, let alone have her driver's license. I just need to know you can get them where they need to go if that happens. You're both listed as family and authorized to give care to my daughter, but Payton doesn't have any identification. She'll need you."

The uneasiness in his chest doubled in strength, stealing his breath for a long moment. "Are you sure you should leave her here? Why not take her with you or wait to go on any trips until she's older? Jesus, Eric."

Compassion filled his brother's gaze and Gabe swallowed hard, looking away. He hated that look with a passion, but he knew as long as he couldn't move on from his daughter's death, it would always be there.

He should at least try to act normal, but he honestly didn't think he had it in him.

"We're going because Brandy's trying to get pregnant, but she's been having difficulty. She managed to a few months ago but she had a miscarriage. It was her third. She has a long day of appointments tomorrow and wants Ailani with her, and we both want to take her and Tai out. We're going to have a nice dinner, and then let the girls go shopping Saturday, and then we'll all go to a show that night. It has to be this weekend, because of the appointments, and that's no place for Ariel to be all day. And they desperately need a break from their reality, Gabe."

"Shit. I didn't know all of that was going on."

"They didn't want anyone to know. They're both torn up about it, and they both need our support. And I think, as much as they love Ariel, the last thing they need is a pint-sized reminder of everything they've lost—especially if the news is bad at Brandy's appointments."

He nodded absently. "I agree with you. I didn't understand, but I do now. I'll answer my phone if Payton calls, I promise."

"I don't anticipate her needing to call you. She said she'll call one of the mated pairs if she has a question or just needs help in general. I just needed to know you'll answer the phone if for some reason she needs you to take them somewhere. I think we'll all be praying she won't need to."

Gabe hadn't prayed since before Mackenzie passed away, but he thought this might be enough to make him send one skyward. "I know I haven't been the most present or active person in Ariel's life, but I promise I won't let you down, Eric."

His brother clapped a hand to his shoulder. "I know your reasons, and I've respected them. And I also know you'll do anything for her, so I don't need your promise, but thanks for giving it. Now I'll let you get out of here like I know you've been itching to do since you first pulled up. Just know that one day in the future, I won't let you escape so easily. Ariel needs her uncle to be an actual participant in her life, and not just a ghost haunting the sidelines."

Eric turned on his heel without waiting for a reply and

strode toward his house. Mouth tightening, he debated calling him back to argue the point, but in the end, he got in his truck and drove away.

His brother had been more than patient with him these last five months and besides, he'd already known that day was coming.

But he was still going to say a little prayer that he wasn't needed this weekend. He needed a little more time to get his heart and mind in order before he was ready to give Ariel the attention and love she deserved from him.

If he ever could...

CHAPTER 3

PAYTON PACED BACK AND FORTH THROUGH THE LIVING room, Ariel held to her chest, worry and panic eating at her insides. The baby had been a little fussy this morning when Ailani and Eric left. They said she was teething, and Payton assured them it wasn't anything she couldn't handle, but damn if she wasn't slowly losing it.

As the day progressed, Ariel slowly got crankier and crankier. Her fussing turned into crying as she began running a low-grade fever—something else Lani warned her about. She'd given her baby Tylenol, but it hadn't seemed to help much, and now her crying had turned into full on sobs.

And it was ripping Payton's heart right out of her chest.

Ariel was such a happy baby all the time, so this was a complete one eighty from anything she'd ever seen before. Poor baby had a sharp object trying to force its way out of her gums and the people she wanted around her most weren't there to give her the comfort she needed.

Instead, she was stuck with Payton—a virtual stranger, for all intents and purposes—who was bumbling her way through taking care of the crying baby, and probably doing a horrific job of it.

She wanted to throw her head back and scream and cry right along with Ariel.

Bouncing the baby lightly, she pressed a kiss to her forehead, freezing when she felt how hot Ariel's skin was against her lips. Panic doubling, she raced to get the thermometer. This wasn't right. She'd only given her the Tylenol an hour and a half ago, so she shouldn't be so freakin' hot this soon.

Besides, didn't Ailani say it would only be a *low*-grade fever? That sure as shit didn't feel low to her lips.

She gently laid Ariel in her bouncy seat, wincing when it made her cries ratchet up to piercing decibel. Fumbling with the thermometer, she forced her shaking hands to steady. Thankful it was an ear thermometer—because Lord knew, she wouldn't be able to handle a regular one, not with the way Ariel was thrashing and carrying on—she pressed the tip gently into the baby's ear, holding her breath and praying.

That Ariel would hold still long enough for her to take it properly—and that her lips were lying, and she wasn't as hot as she seemed.

She couldn't hear the beeping noise it made when it was done because of the baby's cries, but she saw the screen flash, and she pulled it out, heart sinking like a stone when she read the screen.

One hundred and three.

She didn't know much, but she knew that was far too high—especially for a baby that had Tylenol in her system.

"Shit, shit, shit," she muttered, her eyes racing to Ariel. "Sorry."

Lord have mercy on her soul, why was she apologizing to a five-month-old baby for cursing in front of her when she couldn't even understand her to begin with? That was some next level shit right there.

She was way too flustered. She needed to calm the hell down and actually use the brain God gave her. Because she might be a blonde, but she wasn't as ditzy as she was acting, she really wasn't. At least, she never had been before.

Inhaling deeply, she tried to focus, as much as she could with Ariel screaming so loudly. Eric and Lani would never forgive her if something happened to Ariel.

And she'd never forgive herself.

Mind racing, she debated checking her temperature again, but she shook her head, discarding that. It would just waste precious time, because she knew it was right. Ariel actually held still while she took it, and besides, she *felt* that hot to the touch.

"I'll pick you back up in a second, baby girl. I promise."

Sprinting to the phone, she grabbed the cordless and rushed into the kitchen, where a list of phone numbers was stuck to the fridge. She thought briefly for a moment about calling one of her clansmen, but she thought Ariel needed to see her pediatrician, so that meant there was only one person she could call.

Trying to steady her fingers, she punched out the number for Gabe's phone, sinking her teeth into her bottom lip as she listened to it ring. It was killing her to not have Ariel in her sight, or better yet, in her arms right now, but she'd never be able to hear him if she was in the room with the baby. Even now, she had to press her ear hard to the receiver to hear it ringing.

She'd almost given up hope of him answering when his gruff voice came over the line.

"Hello? Payton? What's wrong?"

Relief that he picked up made it hard for her to speak,

and she cleared her throat, hoping to loosen her vocal chords. "I think we need to get Ariel to the doctor. Can you come get us?"

"What was that? I can barely hear you. Dammit, what's wrong with Ariel?"

"Can you just come now? I'll explain once you're here."

"Fuck! I still can't hear you. Listen, I'm coming right over, but if this is a serious emergency, don't wait for me. Call 911, got it?"

He hung up before she could reply, and she shook her head as she set the phone down. Ariel was screaming fit to wake the dead, so he hadn't heard a word she said, but the end result was what she wanted, so she didn't care.

Rushing back into the room, she slung the diaper bag over her shoulder and picked the baby up. Her crying instantly quieted, turning into heartbreaking whimpers as she snuggled into Payton's arms. A lump grew in her throat as she paced slowly back and forth, humming a nameless song as she rocked her.

Should she have called 911? Was Ariel's temperature high enough for that? She didn't think so, but hell, what did she know?

She didn't have kids of her own. She was the oldest of nine siblings, and she'd helped raise all of them, so it wasn't like she was clueless when it came to babies. But that was a thousand years ago—long before thermometers, Tylenol, or hell, even decent doctors as the modern world knew existed.

So much had changed since then. Holding and caring for Ariel came like second nature to her, but a century was long enough that it mooted all of the experience she acquired before being cursed.

Moving to the front window, she watched, waiting for Gabe to show up. She knew he lived on the other side of the lake, but it still wasn't very far at all, because Aurora Falls was small. And she wanted to be ready to go when he got here. The car seat was already by the door, but she wasn't going to put Ariel in it until it was time to go.

Holding the baby seemed to soothe her at least a tiny bit, so she wasn't putting her down until she had to.

Barely a minute had passed before she saw Gabe's bright red Chevy tearing down the drive. He slammed on the brakes, the huge truck skidding to a stop, and her heart squeezed as she rushed to the door.

Even over Ariel's crying, she'd heard the panic in his voice. She hated that her call was worrying him—or possibly giving him horrible flashbacks to when he lost his daughter —but it couldn't be helped.

He was already nearly at the door when she yanked it open, and relief replaced some of the worry in his gaze as he took in the fact that Ariel was seemingly okay, although she'd begun crying softly again.

"What's wrong?" he asked, his liquid brown eyes meeting hers before he looked quickly at the baby again. "She was screaming so loudly that I couldn't understand a word of what you said."

"She's teething, and Ailani and Eric said that she could have a low-grade fever with that. She's gotten fussier and fussier all day, and when I took her temp, she had the fever they warned me about, so I gave her baby Tylenol. But she kept getting more and more agitated, and her fussiness turned to screams. And when I felt her forehead again, she seemed even warmer, so I took her temp. It was a hundred and three, and I just gave her Tylenol an hour and a half ago. That can't be right, right? That's when I called you. I'm sorry, but I panicked, and I think she needs to go to the doctor, so I had to call you—"

"Hey," he said gently, interrupting her rapid-fire flow of words. "Take a deep breath and try to calm down. I'm here, and you did the right thing. She'll be okay. Her pediatrician is probably closed, but we can take her to the urgent care. Everything's gonna be okay."

Inhaling deeply, she let it out nice and slowly, trying to calm her pounding heart. He kept repeating that Ariel was going to be okay, so she decided to try to take him at his word.

She started to crouch down and put Ariel in her car seat but paused as he reached out, using the towel draped over her shoulder to wipe the baby's nose. When he was done, he pressed his palm to her forehead for a moment before running his hand down her bright red curls—and then he yanked his hand away like touching her physically hurt him.

He cleared his throat as he held a hand up to stop her from putting her in the seat. "It'll be easier if I put the seat in the truck first, since I don't have a car seat base in there. She's snotty, but I'm not sure if it's because she has a cold or if it's from all the crying she's done. She is too warm though, especially after Tylenol, you're right about that. Don't look like that. I told you she'd be okay, and I meant it. You have everything you need?"

"Yeah. Let's go. I won't be able to take a full breath until a doctor says she's okay."

"That's a feeling I know well," he muttered as he picked up the car seat and motioned her outside.

Her heart clenched again as she thought about *why* he knew that feeling well, and she had to suck in a breath to keep from losing it. She felt guilty all over again for calling him a jerk in her head.

He certainly wasn't acting like a jerk right now. He was

every inch the caring, worried uncle in that moment. And instead of getting snippy with her and acting like she was a bother—like he had every other time she'd been around him —he was doing his best to calm her fears, and he was being kinder than she'd known he could be in the process.

Focusing on the baby she was holding, who was increasingly becoming more restless as her cries escalated once more, she hurried to the truck. Gabe rushed in front of her, yanking the back door open and quickly securing the car seat before he stepped back, taking the diaper bag from her.

Payton buckled Ariel in, wincing as the baby cried louder when she put her in the seat. Once she was done, she climbed in beside her, looking at Gabe.

"I'll ride back here with her. She hates being put down right now, and I want to try to comfort her as much as I can."

Nodding, he glanced at Ariel once more, and when he closed the door, she saw the worry he was trying so hard to hide from her. He was acting cool and calm, trying his best to ease her fears, but she could tell that inside, he was worried sick.

And the fact that he was trying so hard... well, that more than anything showed her the man he really was inside. It was just a small glimpse into the man he'd been before tragedy tore his life apart, into the man he still was under the gruff exterior and the asshole words he said sometimes.

But even just that tiny peek was enough to let her know how wrong she'd been about him. She knew she'd never actually be friends with him, because he wouldn't allow her to get close enough for that—but she could at least be a little more understanding about why he was always so surly.

CHAPTER 4

Gabe put the diaper bag on the floor by the front door, following Payton slowly inside his brother's house. She gently set the car seat down by the couch, looking like she was holding her breath in case Ariel woke up, but the baby never stirred.

Thank fuck, there was nothing seriously wrong with his niece. He never would have been able to handle that. The doctor said it was just a cold, and that on top of her teething meant she was miserable. He'd given them a prescription for cough syrup if she needed it, and told them to keep up the Tylenol, as well as other instructions for getting her fever down.

All of which Gabe remembered well from being Mackenzie's dad, but Payton had literally grabbed a notepad and pen and took copious notes. It was clear she took her role of caretaker for Ariel seriously, and that relieved his mind, but still—he was hesitant to leave.

She looked exhausted. And he knew the moment she tried to relax or get some rest, Ariel was going to let her know just how much she wouldn't allow that.

It felt like a fist squeezed his heart painfully as he looked at his niece. His demons were stirring in his mind, and he knew he'd pay for spending so much time with her, but he couldn't leave.

Not yet, anyway—although what was left of his splintered heart would shatter as surely as the sun rose and set every day.

"Why don't you sit down and rest? I'll scrounge us up something to eat for dinner."

Eyebrows high, she glanced over at him, mouth opening and closing a few times before she found her voice. "You're staying?"

He shrugged, trying to look casual, but his racing heart as he glanced from her to Ariel and back told him he was anything but. "Taking care of a sick or teething baby is exhausting work, let alone one who's going through both at the same time. I'm here and I have nothing better to do tonight. I can help. Besides, when's the last time you ate?"

Yeah, nothing better to do than work on plans for a new building when the deadline's approaching fast.

He pushed the mocking voice aside. Payton—no, *Ariel*— was more important than his job. He could take one night to take care of them instead of work.

He refocused on Payton, watching as she shrugged sheepishly. "Breakfast, I think. I was too focused on Ariel to worry about eating."

"See? You need to eat and rest a little bit, or you'll be worthless to her. Babies can sense that shit quick."

She bit her bottom lip for a moment before nodding. "Okay. Thank you, Gabe. Just... no leftovers, okay? And don't tell Ailani I said that," she added hastily.

Shaking his head, he chuckled softly. "I won't. If I'm being truthful, I agree with you on that. I'll find us something else instead. Go sit on the couch and try to relax."

She flashed a smile at him, her light blue eyes grateful,

before staring down at the baby again, like she had to check to make sure she was okay one more time before she let herself be for just a moment.

Gabe let his eyes rove over her, noticing her in a way he hadn't allowed himself to before, not even once in the time he'd known her. All he'd allowed himself to notice was that she was cute—but the reality was, she was far more than just cute.

She was tall for a woman. He was six foot three, and she came up just past his chin. She had long blonde hair that fell in a silky waterfall to her waist, the pale shade high-lighted with darker golden streaks throughout. Her eyes were a light, sky-blue, set above a pert nose and full, infinitely kissable lips.

Unease stirred through him at the thought of her mouth, but he still couldn't keep himself from sliding his gaze down her body. She was wearing a figure-hugging shirt, and his lips quirked as he read the words scribbled across her chest—Mermaids Do It Better. Her shirt was black and the writing was bright pink, drawing his eyes straight to her chest. Swallowing painfully around a suddenly dry throat, he took in her snug jeans, letting his eyes drop to her sneaker clad feet before he reversed the course his eyes had taken until he was gazing at her face again.

His blood quickened as his body stirred, and disgust filled him, finally allowing him to break the spell she'd unknowingly cast over him. What the hell was he thinking, letting himself check her out like that, let alone getting so lost in just looking at her?

He hadn't been with a woman since Mackenzie got sick —and just wording it that way made him sick to his stom-ach. Clearing his throat, he whistled softly for Triton and Pippi, opening the back door so the dogs could go out.

Following them outside, he hooked his hands on his hips and inhaled deeply, trying to banish the heavy knot in his gut.

If he was going to stay even for a little bit to help her with Ariel, he needed to nip this sudden attraction in the bud. It was going to be hard enough to be around his niece—he couldn't add thoughts of her beautiful caretaker to it. The guilt of it all would eat him alive as his heart burned to ashes because the little baby he was taking care of was Ariel and not his own Mackenzie.

It was incredibly unfair to Ariel, he knew that—the fact that he had to keep his distance because she wasn't his daughter. It was how he felt, but he never claimed it was rational. Neither was the fact that he already felt guilty for just noticing a woman was attractive.

But in his mind, every slice of happiness he carved out, every time he smiled or laughed, every time he lived instead of just existed—it was a slap in the face to his daughter. The light of his life. His everything.

If she couldn't have those things, why should he?

He knew it wasn't logical. And he knew his daughter would absolutely hate that he felt that way.

But he couldn't help it. It was how he felt, and he didn't know if it was even possible to change it.

When he felt like he had his thoughts and emotions in check, he opened the door to let the dogs in, and then he followed. His lips quirked, the sensation as alien as it always felt, when he noticed that Payton was curled up on the couch, one hand tucked underneath her cheek, the other resting lightly on the car seat as she dozed.

That was good for two reasons—one, she clearly needed the rest; and two, it meant he didn't have to interact with her just yet.

He wanted to have a chance to shore up his crumbling walls just a little bit. She was slipping through already, and he had to put a stop to it.

Just before he turned to head to the kitchen, his eyes fell on the shimmering scale mark on the underside of her right forearm. He stared at it for a long moment and then clenched his jaw tightly as he walked into the kitchen.

He'd seen it the first time they met, and thanks to Eric and Ailani, he knew exactly what it meant. And he was going to keep on doing what he'd been doing from the moment he saw it—continue to pretend it didn't exist to him.

Because it shouldn't. The witch, the fates, whatever they wanted to call it, had screwed up royally when they decided he should be the one to see hers. He wasn't good for her in any way.

And that was what being able to see that mark meant— he was the only one who could see it, and that made him her mate. The one who could break the curse for her.

But he couldn't be her mate. He couldn't be her anything other than what he already was—her best friend's brother-in-law; someone she saw casually in passing, but who meant nothing to her.

CHAPTER 5

PAYTON STIRRED AS SHE HEARD THE FRONT DOOR CLOSE, blinking her eyes open with surprise. She couldn't believe she fell asleep, and at a time like this. Heart jumping in her throat, she looked down at Ariel to find her sleeping peacefully, drool dribbling down her chin.

Thank God the baby was okay. She couldn't let herself sleep like that, not when Ariel was sick and teething like she was.

The sound of plates and silverware tinkling got her attention, and she sat up, running a hand through her long hair. She'd totally forgotten that Gabe was still there. She guessed it wasn't such a bad thing that she fell asleep, then, since she wasn't alone in caring for the baby at the moment, but guilt still welled up inside her.

Standing, she stretched her tired body, glancing down at Ariel one more time before making her way to the kitchen. She wanted to bring her with her, but she didn't want to take the chance that she'd wake her up, either. Poor baby needed some rest.

Stopping in the doorway, she watched as Gabe set cans of Coke by their plates, raising an eyebrow when she saw the box of pizza sitting in the middle of the table. He turned and caught her expression, shrugging as he gestured for her to sit down.

"I worried if I tried to cook, the noises would wake Ariel up. I figured I'd order a pizza and run out to get it from the driver before they rang the bell. It's half pepperoni, half cheese, in case you don't like toppings."

She smiled as she sat down, popping the top on her Coke and taking a sip. "I like it all, but cheese is my favorite. Thanks for doing this."

Opening the box, he gestured for her to take a slice before helping himself. "I figured you wouldn't eat if I didn't make sure you had something. I remember what it's like to be by myself with a sick or teething infant. I was the same as you, until I figured out that if I didn't take care of myself, I wasn't doing her any favors."

Her breath caught at how he casually mentioned his daughter, and she chewed slowly, wondering if he'd retreat into his grumpy shell if she asked any questions. But in the end, her curiosity won out.

"Wasn't your wife around to help?" she asked quietly, figuring it might go over better if she started with Mackenzie's mom, rather than asking about his daughter right off.

He grimaced as he swallowed his bite, his eyes hardening as he frowned. "That bitch never wanted anything to do with Mackenzie. She hated that she got pregnant to begin with, because she was scared of ruining her figure, and once Mackenzie was born, she stayed away from her. I can count on one hand the amount of times she even held her."

When he called his ex-wife a bitch, it jarred Payton, but the more he spoke, the more she felt it was justified. She couldn't imagine resenting a pregnancy because it might ruin her figure, and she couldn't imagine not wanting anything to do with the baby once it was born.

"That's awful," she replied softly, compassion for Mackenzie welling up inside her.

"I handled it fine for myself. I loved Mackenzie and made sure she knew it. But it was hard, once she got older and started asking why her mommy didn't love her. I filed for a divorce after the first time she asked me that. I'd been holding out hope, praying Julie would come around, thinking my daughter was better off with both of her parents. But after that, I realized she wasn't. All she needed was me, and all having her mom around did was make her wonder what she'd done to make her mom not love her."

Heart clenching, she took a sip of her drink, trying to control her emotions. She thought she might hate Julie in that moment. What kind of person, what kind of *mother*, neglected their child so much that they were left wondering what they'd done to make them so unlovable?

"She was lucky to have you, Gabe. Things could have been worse for her, but she had you in her corner, loving and protecting her fiercely."

Clearing his throat, he pushed his plate away, his dark brown eyes troubled as he looked at her. "Sorry. I don't usually talk about this stuff. I don't know why I did now."

"Maybe because you *haven't* talked about it. We all need someone to talk to every now and then. Otherwise, it explodes all over the ones around us when we can't keep the lid closed on the box we shoved it in anymore."

He went quiet for a moment, his eyes narrowed as he studied her, and she took the moment to return the gesture. Gabe was a good-looking man, she'd always known that. He was tall with dark brown hair that was currently a mess around his face from where he'd run his fingers through it repeatedly while they were at the urgent care.

His eyes were a dark brown that looked soft and liquid in that moment, and not the hard, cold gaze she once thought he had. His nose was straight and strong, and he had a closely trimmed beard highlighting lips far too sensual for a man.

Her eyes dropped to where his elbows were resting on the table, his biceps bunched up and straining the seams of his t-shirt. Eric made a comment once about how all Gabe did was work, but it was clear to her that he took the time to work out, too.

Yeah, she'd always known he was a gorgeous man, but seeing firsthand the fierce protectiveness he had toward his daughter, seeing just how much he loved her, made him go from a good-looking guy to sexy as hell in her eyes.

"Maybe you're right," he replied softly. "Not talking about any of it was the only way I could deal with it for a long time, though."

Her eyes raced to meet his, relief filling her that he was giving her a distraction from her thoughts. The last thing she needed to do was become truly attracted to him or, God forbid, get attached. He wasn't her mate, so an attraction between them could go nowhere.

And she didn't *want* it to go anywhere.

Liar.

Uncomfortable with her train of thought, she took a drink as she forced herself to focus on their conversation. "Everyone copes with hard situations differently. It doesn't make our methods wrong. But sometimes, what used to work doesn't anymore, and we have to find new ways to handle old stuff."

He cocked his head, studying her so closely, she was

half worried he could see straight into her soul. "Is that what you had to do for the past thousand years? Find new ways to cope?"

Breath stalling, she stared at him with wide eyes for a long moment until she could find her voice. "What do you mean?" she asked cautiously.

One side of his mouth curled up as a faint gleam of amusement appeared in his eyes. "I mean, since you were cursed to be a mermaid. Eric and Ailani already told me all about it."

She wasn't sure how she felt about this dark, sometimes asshole, sometimes compassionate man knowing her secrets, but she guessed she understood why he was told. "And you didn't freak out when they told you?"

He chuckled, the sound rusty and awkward, like he hadn't laughed in a very long time. "I did at first. I thought they were both crazy and needed help, but we went to the lake and Ailani showed me. It's still hard to believe, though, even after seeing it with my own eyes."

Shaking her head, she smiled wryly as she pushed her plate back, so she could lean in. "It was hard to believe for a long time for me, too, and I was living it. I still am, actually. To answer your question, though, for me, staying hopeful and not losing my optimism is how I've managed to survive. Each of us clansmen have our own methods.

"Ailani, for example, had to shut herself down, basically. She pulled away from the whole clan except me and Tai, and she refused to even search for a mate. She hadn't even been into town until after she met Eric. It was the only way she could cope, because more disappointment would have wrecked her. For myself, what'll wreck me is if I ever let myself give up hoping. I might not see it now, but there's an end to all this for me. One day, my mate will come along and break the curse, and then I can live on the surface. I won't be forced into the lake against my will. If I let go of that hope... that's when I'll lose myself."

Something that looked like unease mixed in with guilt flashed through his dark eyes, and she felt her brow twitch as he shifted uncomfortably on his chair. Something about her words struck something inside him, but she wasn't sure what.

Maybe because she'd help onto her hope for a thousand years and he felt like he hadn't? She wasn't sure, but he couldn't compare their situations. They were totally different. Yeah, she might have survived a thousand years as a mermaid, spending most of her time in a cave deep in the lake, with her optimism intact—but she hadn't lost a child.

That would break her in a heartbeat. She had no doubts about that.

"It's different for everyone," she said softly, reaching across the table to place her fingers gently on his arm. A wave of heat washed over her as her middle clenched, and his arm tensed underneath her fingers. Uncomfortable with the way her body responded, she cleared her throat as she pulled her hand back. "You can put two people in the exact same situation and they'll probably react differently—and neither one is right or wrong. And you can't even begin to compare people in different situations."

Before he could reply, Ariel woke in the other room, her initial fussing quickly turning into cries. Payton's head whipped toward the sound, but not before she saw relief fill his gaze. She turned back when he spoke, his voice abrupt and his gaze betraying no feelings whatsoever.

"You go get her. I'll clean up and put the leftovers away."

She searched his eyes for a moment before nodding,

standing up and making her way to the baby. He was probably relieved to get away from her and her unwanted advice and gentle lecturing, and she couldn't blame him. She'd want away too, if she was him.

But his tone of voice told her it would always be one step forward and two steps back with him.

Not that she wanted to move forward. She didn't. At all.

Liar.

CHAPTER 6

FOLDING HIS ARMS ACROSS HIS CHEST, GABE LEANED ON the doorway, watching as Payton paced back and forth with Ariel, trying her best to calm the upset baby. He hated that his niece was sick and in pain, but he was beyond grateful that she'd interrupted them.

Guilt welled up in his chest again and he tried to push it back down. He never thought he'd feel that emotion when it came to Payton, but when she told him in her sweet, soft voice that she held onto her hope because she'd lose herself without it—that she might not be able to see the end but it was there somewhere, and she just had to wait on her mate to find it—the guilt nearly overwhelmed him.

When he decided that he wasn't going to say a word about probably being her mate, he hadn't been thinking about what she'd gone through—or the fact that finding her mate was the only way to break the curse for her.

No, he'd been a selfish dick and only thought about himself.

Shaking his head slightly, he ran a hand over his face. That wasn't entirely true. He'd been thinking about both of them. He didn't deserve to be happy, not after everything that happened, and someone as bubbly and peppy as

Payton... he was dark these days, all hard planes and sharp edges. He'd make her miserable, and she'd probably do the same to him.

It was best for both of them if he kept the fact that he could see her scale marking to himself.

He still thought that, but what he hadn't been thinking about was how he held the key to breaking her curse. A thousand years... he could hardly fathom how long she'd been trapped under the curse, chained in the lake, only able to walk on land for roughly three days a month.

Her strength was unfathomable to him. He'd have lost his mind a long, long time ago. Yet she remained hopeful, patiently waiting for her mate to come along and break the curse.

And there her mate was, standing across the room from her, able to break her curse now—but he never had any intention of doing it, despite the guilt creeping up his throat and slowly choking him.

Surely, he wasn't the only mate for her, right? It made no logical sense for him to be the only one. One person, in the whole of forever, who could break the curse. No. There had to have been more in the past, and there were more in her future. Him not claiming her as his mate wasn't the end for her. She'd find someone else who could break her out of her prison.

And if he suddenly wanted to smash the unnamed asshole's face in, well, he wasn't going to admit it to anyone —even himself.

Ariel's cries reached an earsplitting decibel and he winced, watching while panic crossed Payton's features. She was trying so hard to comfort the baby, but she was becoming more and more frazzled the longer it took, and it was clear that Ariel was reacting to that.

He couldn't stand there and watch this anymore, but even though he knew what he had to do, a heavy knot coiled in his gut and a cold sweat broke out on his skin. The one and only time he held her wrecked him for weeks after, and he knew this time would be no different.

But he couldn't stand there and be the selfish bastard he'd turned into after Mackenzie died—not when he could help Payton and, most importantly, Ariel.

Your daughter would be ashamed of you for not helping before this.

Didn't he fucking know it, but until that moment, he'd never had an urge to change who he'd become after her death.

Inhaling deeply enough that he thought his lungs were going to pop, he held it for a moment and then breathed it out slowly as he walked forward. "Here, let me try."

Payton's light blue eyes widened as her footsteps faltered in front of him. "You want to hold her? Are you sure?" she asked, raising her voice so he could hear her over Ariel's cries.

Nodding, he inhaled deeply again and simply head his arms out as his reply. He was worried if he tried to speak, the words would come out shaky and strained. It was clear she already knew this was a big deal for him—*thanks, Eric and Ailani*—but he didn't have to let her know how big of a deal it was.

She looked at him skeptically, but she came closer, willingly surrendering Ariel into his arms. He swore his heart stopped the moment he held her. Ariel's cries quieted for a moment as her big green eyes blinked up at him, probably wondering who the hell the strange man holding her was.

Fuck. How did he let it get to the point where his niece didn't know him apart from a stranger?

Because you're a selfish jerk who was only concerned with how you felt around her—and not with how much she needs all of her family in her life.

A burst of pain erupted in his heart, and the sensation sparked a flashback. For a moment, he wasn't looking down at Ariel, with her bright red curls, pale skin, and big green eyes—he was looking at Mackenzie, with her wispy, straight brown hair, darker skin, and brown eyes.

And he mourned the loss of his little girl even more fiercely than he usually did in that slice of time.

But then he blinked and the baby he was holding was Ariel again, and he resolved to see her for herself from there on out. He owed that much to her—and so much more, for being an absentee uncle her whole life.

Ariel was tiny, but although she looked delicate, her weight in his arms was solid and reassuring. And when her eyes filled with tears and she let out another wail, he felt his lips quirk with amusement. There was nothing delicate about her lungs.

Swaying her back and forth, he crooned to her, thankful he'd just washed his hands. Sliding his finger just inside her mouth, he rubbed it gently against her gums, his smile stretching wider as she quieted, blinking up at him as the tears slowly dried in her green eyes.

"That's amazing," Payton breathed, like she was scared if she spoke in a normal voice, she'd break the spell and make Ariel cry again. "I never would have thought to do that. I tried to give her the teething toys, but she showed no interest in them."

"Sometimes they want something more than a rubbery plastic toy. I used to do this with Mackenzie, too. It was the only way she didn't cry because she had zero interest in the toys."

She sucked in a breath at his mention of his daughter, and he knew it was because he never talked about her—not with her, and not with anyone, really. He waited for the pain of doing so to bring him to his knees, but instead of soul searing agony, he felt the warmth of remembrance wash over him.

That was an unexpected change, but it was a welcome one. He often felt guilty because he couldn't talk, or sometimes even think, of her without feeling like he couldn't breathe while the pain of losing her tore him to shreds.

So, while he thought about her often, he rarely talked about her, and he hated that. Maybe he was turning a corner, one where he could honor her memory like she deserved.

He probably wasn't, but he could take a page out of Payton's book and hope, right?

"I'll go get a bottle made for her. She's most likely hungry by now."

He nodded as relief washed over him. He'd been worried she'd ask questions about his daughter. And while he wanted to talk about her, he wasn't sure he was ready yet.

He kept his eyes on Ariel until Payton turned away and then he looked up, tracing them over her body. Her long hair teased her ass while she walked, and he swallowed hard as his gaze dropped to the globes, moving tantalizingly with each step and highlighted to perfection in her snug jeans.

Tearing his eyes away, he looked back at Ariel. "I need a distraction. What do you say we get this diaper changed and get into some pajamas while your aunt Payton fixes you a bottle, hmmm?"

She smiled around his finger and he felt his heart swell with love as he carried her to her bedroom. He should have done this a hell of a lot sooner. Once he got past that initial shock of pain, he found that he was more or less okay. And he'd basically missed the first five months of her life because he'd had his head stuck so far up his ass that he couldn't see her for the amazing, gorgeous baby she was.

He quickly changed her clothes, relief filling him when she fussed a little but didn't cry. They got back to the living room just as Payton walked in, and she smiled when she saw he'd changed her. She held her arms out for the baby and he quickly shook his head.

"I'll feed her. Can you put her bib on for me, though?"

Her eyebrows rose but she nodded as she smiled, quickly putting the bib on and handing him the bottle. Walking over to the rocking chair, he sank down, holding the nipple to her bow shaped lips and smiling as she immediately latched on, suckling hungrily despite the fact that her gums hurt her.

It took a moment, but he realized he'd smiled so much that day that it was starting to feel not quite as weird.

"You're a total natural at that. You're amazing with her."

Glancing up, he arched an eyebrow at her. It took her a second, but she flushed as she squeezed her eyes closed, and when she opened them, there was regret lurking in the sky-blue depths.

"I'm sorry. Of course you know what you're doing with her. I didn't think before I spoke."

"It's okay," he replied softly, glancing down at Ariel, watching as her eyes started to slide closed before looking back at Payton. "You never met Mackenzie, and you and I never really spent any time together before this. I wouldn't expect you to remember all the time."

She exhaled softly, biting her lower lip for a moment. "I

feel like I should remember, though. Will you tell me about her?"

He'd been looking at Ariel again, but his gaze shot back up to hers. Did he want to talk about his daughter with her? Honestly, he wanted to, and he'd just been thinking that he needed to talk about her with someone—he just didn't know if he was strong enough yet.

But he'd never know if he didn't at least try. With that in mind, he inhaled deeply, trying to brace himself for this conversation.

"She was beautiful and the light of my life. I thought I knew what love was before her—I mean, I love my brother and my parents, and I thought I loved Julie until we got married and she turned into a cold bitch—but I really had no clue. Mackenzie taught me what it means to really, truly love.

"She was such a happy baby, and that didn't change as she got older. The only time she didn't have a smile on her face was when Julie was around, but the moment we divorced, and I got her out of that toxic environment, Kenzie went back to being all smiles. She loved puppies, and she's the one who talked Eric into adopting Triton. She loved butterflies and rainbows, and The Little Mermaid was her favorite movie." He stopped, smiling wryly at Payton. "Ironic, right? That's how the dog got his name. She was a sweetheart, and wise beyond her years. Especially at the end."

His throat tightened, the last few words coming out hoarse and gritty. He was fighting to get ahold of his emotions, and the soft sound of compassion Payton let out didn't make it any easier.

"She sounds like an amazing little girl."

Nodding, he cleared his throat, waiting on the pain to

recede. Because, surprisingly, he didn't want to stop there. He wouldn't normally bring up the dark time when she fought for her life, but for some insane reason, he wanted to let Payton in. He wanted her to know just *how* amazing his little girl had been.

"She was. When she got sick… when the doctor said she had leukemia, I thought they got it wrong. I was positive they had. There was no way, abso-fucking-lutely no way, my sweet, gorgeous little girl had cancer. Her light burned too brightly to be dimmed with an illness like that. But, like with everything else, she took it in stride, and she fought. For a long, torturous year, she fought."

His voice cracked and Payton stood, walking quickly over to him. Crouching by the chair, she put her hand on his arm and rubbed gently, and he glanced down, watching her touch him while he fought to regain control over his emotions.

"You don't have to talk about that part if you don't want to, Gabe."

She was giving him the perfect out—but the hell of it was, he didn't want to take it. He wanted to see this through.

And it honestly freaked him the hell out that he wanted to tell her all of this so badly. His walls were crumbling around her like they were made of paper and paste, not the solid brick and mortar he'd always thought they were.

What the hell was happening to him?

CHAPTER 7

Payton looked up at Gabe from where she was crouched next to him, her heart in her throat. The pain in his liquid brown gaze made her want to take him in her arms and hug him tightly—and she would have, if he hadn't had his arms full with Ariel.

Her heart ached, and she didn't know if she was feeling his pain or if it was her own. She wished she'd been able to meet Mackenzie, and the fact that she'd battled cancer so young, ultimately losing her war, was heartbreaking.

"She was a warrior," Gabe said softly, bringing her attention back to the present. "She fought the cancer with every ounce of her being, and even though she was sick and in so much pain, she rarely lost the smile on her face. And in her last few days, she imparted all of the wisdom she had on me and Eric. She wouldn't be happy if she knew who I turned into after she died, but it damned near killed me to lose her. I wanted to crawl into that grave with her."

Tears filled her eyes and she blinked them back, her fingers tightening on his arm. "Gabe..."

Giving his head a quick shake, he looked at her and tried to force a smile, the gesture looking more like a grimace. "She was seven when she died. She would have been eight the following month. It's been three years now, and I try to imagine her as an eleven-year-old, but I have a hard time with it. She's forever frozen at seven, taken from this world far too early."

Stopping, he cleared his throat and scooted to the edge of the chair. She stood and backed away, watching with concern as he put the bottle on the table and gazed down at Ariel for a moment before looking back up at her.

"She should sleep for most of the night. You know what to do if her fever comes back, and if she wakes up teething, try what I did. I'm gonna go lay her down and then I need to go home. I have work to do."

He turned and disappeared down the hallway, and she wrapped her arms around herself as she waited for him to come back. She felt like she should say something, but she didn't have a clue what. She was just going to have to wing it and hope she found the right words.

Biting her lip, she waited for him to come back and when he did, she stepped forward. "Gabe—"

"I really have to go. Call me again if you need to."

Before she could get another word out, he was gone. Exhaling, she dropped to the couch, worry welling up inside her. From what Eric and Ailani said, he never talked about Mackenzie, and as glad as she was that he opened up to her, she almost wished it had been to someone else.

She knew how to talk about bad things happening in life, and she was well versed in things like curses—but knowing what to say to a parent in so much pain from the loss of a child was beyond her.

The phone rang and she rushed to answer it, not wanting it to wake the baby. "Hello."

"Pay, how are things? Is Ariel doing okay?"

Her worry instantly turned to how to break the news of

the doctor visit to Ailani without completely freaking her out. Blowing out a breath, she paced the length of the living room, thinking as much as she'd been making the same route, she probably hit her steps three times over that day.

"She's okay," she began, figuring she should start with that first.

"I know that tone of voice, Pay. What happened?"

Trust her best friend to figure out something happened when all she said was, *she's okay.* "She was running a fever even after I gave her some Tylenol. It freaked me out so I called Gabe and he picked us up and took us to the urgent care. The doctor said she has a cold on top of teething and sent us home with baby cough syrup if she needs it, and instructions for if her fever gets high again. I promise you, she's okay."

Ailani gasped and she could hear Eric in the background, asking what was going on. Lord, Payton hated giving them this news, especially since this was the first time they'd left Ariel for more than a few hours at a time.

"My poor baby. Do you need us to come home tonight instead of tomorrow?"

"No, I've got it covered and I promise she's okay. Gabe hung out and helped me with her tonight, and—wait. Tomorrow? I thought you were coming home Sunday."

"*Gabe* hung out and helped with her?" Ailani asked with shock in her voice, nearly speaking over her. "And yeah. The specialist didn't take as long with Brandy as they thought, and while they didn't get great news, it wasn't bad like they feared. We went to the show tonight and had dinner, so we're coming home in the afternoon. Now what's this about Gabe hanging out?"

"I don't know what I would have done without him, Lani. He was calm and quickly eased my fears, getting us to the urgent care in record time," she replied, telling her about the doctor visit and Gabe getting them dinner while she fell asleep. "And as we were talking after dinner, Ariel started fussing and I couldn't get her calm. He took her and got her to stop crying, and then he fed her before leaving."

Silence stretched out on the line for a moment before her friend spoke again, the shock still in her voice. "Gabe *held* her? And *fed* her? And he actually *talked*?"

"He did *what*?" Eric asked in the background, sounding even more shocked than Lani, if that was possible.

Payton waited patiently for Ailani to answer him, her lips curled up in a smile. She understood the shock they felt—hell, theirs was probably greater than hers, since they knew Gabe a lot better than she did.

"I can't believe he held her. He hasn't done that since right after she was born."

Her eyebrows raised. "Seriously? I knew he didn't hold her much, but I didn't know it'd been that long."

"He's only held her once," Lani replied, her voice soft and sad. "And his eyes were tortured afterward, so we haven't pushed him to hold her more, although Eric wanted to."

A lump of emotion welled up inside her and she cleared her throat, hoping to dispel it. "Well, he not only volunteered this time, but once she was calm and I tried to take her back so I could give her the bottle, he said he wanted to feed her."

"Wow. I wish we hadn't missed that, but I guess if we'd been around, it wouldn't have happened at all. What did he talk to you about?"

"We talked about me being a mermaid and the curse for a bit. Thanks for warning me that he knew, by the way," she said dryly. "And then we talked about Julie and Mackenzie for the rest of the time. He tore out of here pretty fast after talking about his daughter, but I think that's understandable. He still feels her loss deeply."

"What? He talked about his ex *and* Mackenzie? Was he drunk?"

Indignation welled up inside her. "What? Of course not."

"I was kidding! Mostly," Lani muttered under her breath. "He just never talks about them. I've heard him talk about Julie, or the bitch on heels as he calls her, but I think I've only heard him say his daughter's name once."

"He said it hurts too much so he keeps it bottled up inside, but he thought it was time to talk about her to someone. I think holding Ariel might have broken through a wall there. She's like magic."

Ailani scoffed and Payton could practically see her with her eyebrow cocked. "I think maybe you did, too. Even if he wanted to talk about her, he wouldn't have with you if he hadn't felt comfortable enough. You're not without magic of your own, Pay. I've always thought so."

Flushing as a smile curled her lips up, she covered a sudden yawn as exhaustion hit her. She'd had a short nap, but she was already tired again—babies were exhausting.

"Thanks. And I'm glad Brandy and Tai didn't get bad news. You guys still could have stayed longer, though. No harm in having some fun while you're there."

"Well, we went to the show and dinner tonight, and we're still going shopping in the morning before we head home. But I think they're anxious to get back and get to work on making another baby. And since we're still doing everything we talked about, it's not a big deal. You sound exhausted, so I'll let you go. Give Ariel a kiss for me when she wakes up, and make sure you get some rest. Call us if anything else happens, okay?"

Payton agreed and hung up the phone before letting the dogs out one more time. Flounder finally came out of hiding and she scratched behind his ears, walking into the kitchen to make sure he had food and water. He always hid for the first day she was there, and she wondered if he somehow sensed the mermaid in her and it made him nervous.

Walking back to the bedroom, she quickly changed into her pajamas before letting the dogs back in, her mind going over what Ailani said about her having magic. She knew she hadn't meant it in the literal sense, but maybe there was something more to Gabe opening up to her tonight.

And why, for the love of all that was holy, did her mind turn to his sensual mouth when she wondered if there was something more to it? She needed to shut those thoughts down, and quickly.

He wasn't her mate. Her scale marking was in a spot that would be very obvious to the man who could break her curse. If he'd seen it, he would have said something. And since he wasn't her mate, she needed to nip this attraction in the bud.

She couldn't start something with a man who wasn't her intended. She couldn't begin to imagine how horrible that could turn if she met him while she was with Gabe. And speaking of him, he'd had enough heartbreak in his life. She wasn't going to add to it by getting involved with him and then maybe having to dump him for another man.

Sighing, she laid on the bed, lifting her arm and tracing her scale marking. Honestly, as much as the idea of even setting eyes on Gabe yesterday irritated her—she'd gone so far as to wait in the woods until he left Ailani's, after all—

after today, well... she wouldn't mind if he was her mate. At all.

Especially since that would mean she could kiss those irresistible lips any time she wanted to.

She couldn't help snorting at her thoughts, eyes still roving over the iridescent scales on the underside of her right forearm. She must really be getting lonely and desperate if she was starting to think Gabe looked good as a mate.

The truth was... well, she *was* lonely, although she tried to quell any hint of desperation. She always had. Feeling desperate would only lead toward her spiraling in the darkness that stalked her, waiting to pull her under. She didn't want to give in to it, didn't want to be depressed. She liked being happy and always liked the fact that she was naturally optimistic. And she didn't want that to change.

But hell, even back before the clan was cursed, she was lonely. Maybe it was because she grew up in such a large family, but she'd been ready to settle down and start her own even way back then. Most would think that after being saddled with helping to raise so many siblings, she'd want nothing to do with that for a long time, but they'd be wrong.

Oh, she had her time where all she wanted to do was travel and become the best warrior she could be. But even though she was skilled in fighting, being a warrior wasn't the best fit for her. She was a nurturer, first and foremost.

Right before they left for their world travels that last time, she'd decided it was going to be her last journey. The decision hadn't been an easy one, mostly because of Ailani —they'd been best friends since they were very small, and they always had each other's back. She didn't like not being there to help watch her friend's, and she'd known she'd miss her like mad.

But she couldn't let that hold her back from her dream—which was always to be a wife and mother.

Instead of completing the journey and going back home to chase her dream, they were cursed and she was stuck here.

And she never saw her homeland again.

She never would. There was nothing left for her there. Everyone she knew had been dead for a century—all she had was this little town and her best friend.

Who might grow old and die before her very eyes, now that the curse was broken for her and she had a normal life.

Tears pressed against her eyelids and she sniffled, rolling over to turn the lamp off. Jesus. Where did this come from? What happened to holding onto her hope with both hands and fighting tooth and nail against the darkness?

Pressing the heels of her palms against her eyes, she blew out a breath and pushed those thoughts out of her head. She was going to go to sleep, and when she woke up in the morning, she'd be back to her optimistic self.

No more darkness, no more pain, no more wanting things with Gabe that she had no business wanting.

And that was that.

CHAPTER 8

Gabe pulled into Eric's driveway, surprise filling him when he saw his brother's SUV parked by the door. Worry washed over him, and he was coaching himself not to panic when he caught sight of blonde hair out of the corner of his eye.

Looking over, he saw Payton walking into the woods, a backpack slung over her shoulder. Getting out of the truck, he cast another glance at his brother's house before hurrying after her.

"Payton! Wait up."

She turned around, eyebrows raising when she saw him. His breath caught in his chest as she stopped in a pool of sunlight that lit up her light blonde hair and made her sky-blue eyes look even bluer.

Fuck, she was beautiful.

And dammit, he told himself he wasn't going to notice that about her anymore.

"Hey. Is everything okay?" he asked, not sure if he was breathless from the jog over to her or because of that thing he wasn't going to notice anymore.

Her eyebrows twitched, confusion filling her blue eyes as she cocked her head. "Yeah. Why?"

Clearing his throat, he fought to beat back the awareness of her that was washing over him in tidal waves strong enough to bring him to his knees.

"I just saw that Eric and Ailani are home early. Did something else happen with Ariel?"

Her eyes cleared as she shook her head quickly. "Oh. No, she's fine. She seems like she's feeling better today, actually. They just finished up everything they wanted to do early. Brandy's appointments went well, and they did a show and dinner last night and shopping this morning."

"That's good," he replied, relief washing over him at the realization that his niece, as well as his brother and sister-in-law, were all okay. "Why are you out here walking through the woods?"

She grimaced, casting her eyes up at the sky. "I can usually tell when the moon is going to start pulling on us, and it's going to shortly. I was just gonna get close to the lake until it was time to go in. I don't like being very far from it when that happens, because I don't want to not have time to get in the water."

It was surely the guilt of keeping the fact that he could see her scale marking to himself that was responsible for his next words. "Why don't you let me give you a ride? That way you can get there quicker."

Her eyes widened and for a split second, he thought she was going to refuse, but then she nodded with a smile. "Okay. Thanks."

Feeling stunned by that smile—and the little dimple at the corner of her mouth that he hadn't noticed before—he moved aside so she could walk first. They were silent at first as they walked, and then she turned her head to say something just as her foot got caught in a tree root. She started to stumble, and he quickly reached out, grabbing her arm to keep her from falling.

And for the next few moments, the world around him faded away. Sucking in a breath, he watched as, fast as a speeding bullet, the history of her clan flashed before his eyes. Old ships, men and women in primitive Viking clothing, arriving at a new land, setting up temporary camps while they harvested the land's resources to bring back home with them.

And then the witch, Tamsin, falling in love with Bjorn and cursing the whole clan when she found him with another woman and realized he never loved her the way she loved him. The clan cursed to live their lives as merfolk, only able to walk on land during the cycle of the full moon for roughly three days a month.

So much information thrown at him so quickly. No more than a few seconds had passed since he touched her, but he saw it all play out, and it was embedded in his memory now.

"Sorry about that," Payton said breathlessly. "I guess I need to watch where I'm going. Hey, are you okay?"

Clearing his throat, he nodded, refocusing on his surroundings to find her looking at him with worry in her sky-blue eyes. "Yeah, I'm fine. Just worried you'd hurt your-self. You're okay, right?"

She narrowed her eyes, looking like she might question him, but to his eternal relief, she nodded slowly. "Yeah, I'm fine. A little embarrassed at my gracelessness, but physically fine."

She laughed lightly as she spoke, and he couldn't help but chuckle along with her. Like last night, the sound surprised him. He'd forgotten what it was like to laugh, even just a small one like that. It sounded rusty and unused to him, maybe even a little awkward, but to his surprise he found he actually liked the sound of it.

They made the rest of the walk to his truck in silence, and he opened the passenger door for her, his hand automatically going out to help her climb in. Her eyebrows raised as she glanced at it, but she put her hand in his and he sucked in a breath as he helped her inside.

Why did touching her have to feel like this? Like her skin was made for his, like his soul calmed and soared at the same time—like, for that moment in time, their hearts beat in sync?

Jesus. When did he start spouting off poetry shit like that?

Feeling disturbed to his core, he shut the door and went to his side, resolving not to offer to help her next time. His truck was jacked up, yeah, but she was a tall woman and he had step sides. She could manage to get in and out on her own just fine.

He started the truck and just before he began reversing, he noticed Eric standing in his open doorway, watching them. Uneasiness blossomed in his chest, and he wondered how he was going to explain this next time he talked to him. The last thing he wanted was for any of them to get ideas about why he was suddenly showing an interest in Payton.

The lakeshore where he knew the mermaids went wasn't very far, so really, she could have walked easily. None of his actions were making sense to him—not the day before and not today.

And there was that guilt creeping up inside him again. Seeing her history for himself made it more real. It wasn't just a story someone was telling—it was real life. It was *Payton's* life.

And he had the ability to put a stop to the vicious cycle

she was caught in. But instead of getting her out of it, he let it continue, because he'd thought they were better off apart.

No, not *used* to think it. He still thought that—only it was getting harder and harder to remember why.

In only a few minutes, they were nearing the dirt road that led to the lake. Once he parked, he realized he hadn't said what he'd specifically sought her out to say, his mind too consumed with thoughts of her and what the hell he was doing to remember his purpose. But by the time he remembered, she'd already opened her door and started to get out.

Exhaling, he turned his truck off and got out, shoving his keys in his pocket as he met her at the front of the truck. She glanced over at the lake and his chest tightened painfully as the setting sun bathed her in its glow.

"So, um, thanks for the ride. I appreciate it," she said softly as she met his eyes again.

"Any time. Look... I wanted to apologize for how I left yesterday. I should have made sure Ariel stayed asleep and was really okay. Instead I jetted out of there without even giving you a chance to say goodnight. I just—I never talk about Mackenzie. I should, I know, but it's always been too hard. My emotions kind of got the better of me—"

She put her hand on his arm. "Gabe, I understand. I know that was hard for you, and I didn't blame you for leaving or for the way you left. I was just happy you opened up to someone about her. I think you needed that."

Nodding slowly, he blew out a breath, trying and failing to pull himself out of her bright blue gaze. "I think I did, too. I think sometimes that I don't honor her memory well, because it's so fucking hard to talk about her. I should be strong enough to handle the pain. And instead, I'm a weak asshole who snaps and growls at everyone and can barely say his daughter's name."

Payton's breath caught, and she shook her head vigorously as she touched her fingertips to his cheek. "Gabe, no. I told you last night, we all cope in our own ways. And grief is a different monster altogether. You survived the best way you could, and there's nothing wrong with the way you did it."

Reaching up, he caught her hand in his, telling himself to let her go. But in the end, he did the opposite, tightening his fingers around hers. Trying to convince himself he didn't enjoy it as much as he did, he cocked an eyebrow at her.

"Are you saying the way I used to growl at you was okay? I was a jerk to you, Payton. I'm a jerk to everyone, and I don't even mean it half the time. It's just second nature to me now."

"Well, no, I wouldn't say it was okay." Her wry smile softened, turning understanding and kind—and breathtaking. "But I didn't hold it against you, because I knew what you were going through. And no one who knows you will blame you."

"You didn't hold it against me? Even a little?"

She flushed, her cheeks turning a pretty shade of pink. "Okay, maybe a little. I thought you were a total jerk, to be honest. But that doesn't mean I truly held it against you. I knew why, and I understood that part. I just did my best to avoid you. It wasn't like it was hard, seeing as how I can only be on the surface for two or three days a month."

Cocking his head, he studied her, running his gaze over her delicate features before meeting her eyes again. "You tried to avoid me? I didn't know that."

Blush deepening, she shrugged her shoulders sheepishly. "There are only a couple times I purposefully did it. Like when I got to Ailani and Eric's the other day. Your truck was in the driveway, so I waited until you left before I went in."

Guilt and shame washed over him at her admission. He knew he'd been a dickhead to a lot of people since Mackenzie passed, but he hated that he'd made someone as sweet and bubbly as Payton feel like she had to avoid him.

What the hell had he let himself turn into in his grief? The Gabe she was describing, the one he saw in other people's eyes and in the mirror every morning... that wasn't the man he'd been, once upon a time.

And he was really starting to dislike that he'd let himself stray so far from the man he'd always been at his core.

"I'm sorry about that. I wish you'd have come in. I feel like a major asshole, knowing you waiting outside for me to finish dinner before you went in. If I'd known you were there, I would have eaten faster."

She shook her head, her fingers squeezing his. "Don't feel bad. I wasn't out there long—maybe ten minutes, max, but probably less. And I know from talking to Ailani and Eric that you never stay long." She smiled up at him impishly. "Besides, Ailani cooked, so I'm sure you shoved it down as fast as you could so it would be over quicker. I saw the burnt noodles. You probably saved my taste buds from horrific torture by being there."

She mock shuddered and a deep laugh came out of him, surprising him. He'd been chuckling more the past few days, but that was the first true laugh he'd given in a long time.

Three years, to be exact.

As much as he suddenly didn't want to be the man he'd turned into, the thought of changing scared him shitless. The new Gabe was tough, strong, with fortified walls that never let anything pierce his armor. The old Gabe was far too vulnerable to pain—and he didn't want to go back to the man who hurt so badly.

There had to be a compromise between the two he could find.

"She's getting better," he finally replied, pushing his thoughts and—he had to face it—his insecurities to the side. "Eric is too, surprisingly."

She smiled, shaking her head. "Slowly. A little too slowly. I've learned to eat *before* I go to their house. I tried to just fib about it once and then my stomach growled and they busted me. Made me eat. I don't want to do that again. I'm glad that I've gotten a lot of practice in over the years. I love to cook, and it's one of the things I miss when I'm in the lake."

Eyes narrowing, he studied her closely, his mind still stuck on what she said about grief. "Can I ask you a question?"

"Sure. You can ask me anything."

"When you were cursed and forced to stay here, close to Sapphire Lake... did you leave anyone behind at home? Parents, siblings," *—don't say it, Gabe—* "a boyfriend or husband?"

Apparently, his mouth had a mind of its own, even when he was ordering it to stand down.

A look of sadness passed through the light blue depths of her gaze, her eyes telling him she was far away in that moment as she sighed.

"No husband or kids. Not even a boyfriend. I wanted it, though. So badly. This was actually going to be my last journey. I wanted to settle down and have a family. Life gets in the way of everyone's plans though, right?" The corner of her mouth lifted in a slight smile, but it quickly fell away. "I had parents and siblings, though. Nine siblings, actually."

His eyebrows rose, and he pushed away the irrational relief he felt at her saying she hadn't had someone special waiting on her at home so he could focus on the rest of her statement. "Nine siblings? Wow. I can't imagine eight more of Eric running around."

She laughed softly, her eyes still in another time and place, even though they were looking into his. "Yeah, it was a huge family, even for my time. I loved it, though. I was the oldest, so I ended up having a lot of responsibility for the others. I basically helped raise them. I think that's where my desire for a husband and kids of my own comes from. I've always had that desire, but now that I've been away from my family for so long, it's even stronger than it was before."

"So, you have experience with loss, too. A lot of it," he replied softly after a long pause, wondering if he could have dealt with everything better than he had.

Her eyes suddenly sharpened, snapping back to the present, and she shook her head as she studied him. "Oh, no. Don't compare us. Our grief is different. *We're* different, so of course our reactions to it won't be the same. And don't forget that I've had a thousand years to deal with mine. I might be a bit too peppy and optimistic now, but it took a long time to heal from their loss. You've only had three years. You can't compare that to the century I've had."

"I don't think you're too peppy and optimistic," he replied, his voice deep and hoarse as his emotions rose up out of nowhere to strangle him. "I admit, I used to think that, but not anymore. I think the *way* you are is perfect for *who* you are. And don't let anyone, especially my grumpy, pissed off self, make you feel differently."

Her breath caught as her eyes softened, and she stretched up, placing a gentle kiss on his cheek. "Thank you, Gabe," she whispered as she eased away.

His cheek legit fucking tingled where she'd kissed him, the imprint of her mouth burning his skin like she'd branded him. He couldn't say what came over him then—maybe he had his own form of moon madness, because he was powerless to fight the urges overwhelming him.

Placing one hand on her hip, he pulled her into him, reveling in the way she sucked in a breath as her pupils dilated. He untangled their fingers and cupped her cheek before running his fingers into her hair as he lowered his head.

He didn't know what the hell he thought he was doing, but for once, he wasn't going to fight it. He wasn't going to fight *her*.

Instead, he was going to kiss the hell out of her.

CHAPTER 9

PAYTON SWALLOWED HARD AS SHE STARED UP AT GABE, barely breathing. He had one hand on her hip, one tangled in her hair, and he was lowering his head. He was going to kiss her, and even though she'd told herself she couldn't go there with him, she knew she was going to let him.

She was powerless to stop it. Hell, more than that, she craved it. She desperately wanted to know how his lips felt on hers.

When his lips finally touched hers, it felt like the whole universe stopped. So many different sensations exploded in her body, her skin tingling as she reached up and grasped a handful of his t-shirt, clutching tightly.

He moved slowly at first, just brushing his lips against hers for long moments, and then he finally kissed her firmly. She gasped, sucking in a lungful of much needed oxygen. She'd been lightheaded and dizzy from lack of air—or was that because of his kiss?

She honestly didn't know, and she didn't care.

All that mattered was the feel of his mouth against hers.

His hand flexed on her hip as he lightly ran his tongue across her lips, and she whimpered as her core tightened. Opening her mouth, she let him in, meeting his tongue with hers. He kept the kiss gentle, tangling his tongue with hers softly, but she could feel the impatience behind the gesture, could feel the power he was keeping leashed.

She longed for him to set it free, but she knew there wasn't time for that. She could feel the tug of the moon more firmly with every passing moment. She'd have to go into the lake soon—and never had she resented the curse more than in that moment.

Gabe slowly gentled the kiss again until he was passing his lips over hers, and then he finally pulled back. She kept her eyes closed for several long moments, listening to the sound of their harsh breathing.

Finally opening her eyes, she met his gaze, her knees weakening further at the heat she saw in the liquid brown depths. Blinking, knowing she probably looked as dazed as she felt, she willed strength into her limbs.

She shouldn't have let him kiss her, and she knew it would make it that much harder to pull away like she needed to—but damned if it hadn't been worth it.

Honestly, she wasn't sure if it was because she hadn't kissed anyone in hundreds of years or if it was because he was just that good of a kisser, but she knew she'd be thinking about this moment until she was old and grey.

He looked just as stunned as she felt, and neither of them said a word, just gazed into each other's eyes as their breathing slowly calmed. She basked in the moment for as long as she could, but the moon was tugging on her in full force, and she finally let go of his shirt to rub her chest.

His gaze followed her hand, and with a frown he met her eyes again. "What's wrong?"

Smiling faintly, she tried to inhale deeply, but already she felt like she couldn't get enough air. "The curse. I'm starting to have trouble getting oxygen, so I need to get in the lake soon."

His frown deepened. "You better get in, then. I don't like that you can't breathe."

Her smile turned wry as she stepped back. "I don't like it, either. You should go. The other merfolk will be coming soon, and they won't want to get in while you're watching."

Nodding, he ran a hand through his hair. "Okay. Well, um... I'll catch you next time, I guess."

He turned and strode back toward his truck and she couldn't help her chuckle. His eyes and voice had been awkward, like he wasn't sure what to say to the woman he'd just kissed senseless—the same one who had to go a few moments later, because she had to turn into a mermaid or she wouldn't be able to breathe.

Exhaling, she turned and walked around the bend. Once she heard his truck start, she walked over to the woods and quickly disrobed, shoving her clothes in her backpack and leaving it for one of the caretakers to find. Turning, she made her way to the dock and started running, diving into the lake as she reached the end.

The moment she touched the lake water, her legs were replaced by her mermaid tail, and she swam around a bit before making her way to her cave. It was actually Ailani's old place—she couldn't help her snort at the thought of equating the cave to a home—but she'd started staying in it once her friend was living on the surface again.

Pathetic, maybe, but it made her feel like her best friend was still close by—even though she might as well have been on Mars. As far as distance went, they really weren't far from each other, but since she was stuck in the lake, they might as well have been light years apart.

Swimming to a large rock in the back of the cave, she

laid down on it, watching as her long hair slowly floated down to lie beside her. Her thoughts immediately turned toward Gabe, and her fingers reached up to trace her lips.

Damn, what a kiss that had been. Not to mention, the side of him he showed her... When she decided to stay away from him the night before, when she decided she couldn't let herself start anything with him, it had been hard enough then.

But now, after he apologized and then topped it off by kissing the breath right out of her—how was she supposed to stick to her resolve now?

But hell, this was Gabe she was thinking about. He'd changed so quickly that he'd given her whiplash. No doubt, the next time she saw him, he'd go right back to acting how he had before.

The thought made her sad, her chest aching at the idea of him going back to his grumpy, jerk self. But it really was for the best. They shouldn't get involved with each other, and she clearly couldn't be counted on to be the one who kept her distance from him.

Her mind and her heart were at war with each other, and she knew she'd slowly go crazy before the next month was up, so she shut her eyes with determination. Her people could go into a deep sleep until the next full moon, and she was determined to do that. She didn't always, but this time, she *needed* to.

Otherwise the darkness and depression that were always lurking would reach up and grab her at the thought that she couldn't have Gabe like she wanted.

CHAPTER 10

WHAT THE HELL AM I DOING HERE?

Gabe asked himself the question again as he sat on the dock overlooking Sapphire Lake, but just like the other twenty times he asked it, he didn't have an answer.

All he knew was he hadn't been able to get Payton out of his head. He thought about her damned near all day every day, and he dreamed about their kiss at night. She had his insides all twisted up in knots, and he didn't know what the hell to do about it.

He'd thought—hoped, if he was being honest—that his time with her had been an aberration. That he'd go back to being the same Gabe he'd come to know once she left.

Only he hadn't.

He was still a mixture of old him and new him. Hell, he'd even voluntarily gone to Eric and Ailani's for dinner a few times, and if that didn't say something about the change in him sticking, he didn't know what would. Dinner at their house wasn't exactly the most filling and tasteful way to eat a meal.

Exhaling heavily, he looked over at the mountain where the sun was starting to sink. He still didn't think it was a good idea to get involved with Payton, or to admit that he could see her mark—at least, he didn't *think* it was. He was all screwed up inside now. So why the hell had he Googled when the next full moon was and then driven out here to meet her as she came out of the lake?

He didn't have a single fucking clue—all he knew was it had been a need, a compulsion he hadn't been able to ignore.

So, there he was. Waiting on a mermaid he hadn't been able to get out of his head, still wondering why she was implanted in his thoughts so deeply that he couldn't shake her.

The water started rippling and he held his breath as he waited to see if it was her. A few long moments passed before her blonde head popped above the surface, and his heart jumped as he watched her reach up a hand, wiping the water out of her eyes.

She glanced up and came to a stop, the water rippling around her shoulders, her sky-blue eyes widening so much it would have been comical if she wasn't stealing the breath right out of his chest.

"Gabe?" she asked, treading water. "What are you doing here?"

"The truth?"

She nodded. "Of course."

Shrugging, he tried to figure out how to answer that, but he didn't really know that himself. "I don't have a single clue. I just... I had to be here."

Nodding slowly, she eyed him, looking like she wasn't sure what to say now, either. Why did this feel so awkward?

Because you showed up out of nowhere armed with a gut feeling and no plan.

Yeah. That.

He cleared his throat, mind racing for something to say, some way to get them back on the same level they'd been on a month ago. "Do you want to go grab something to eat?"

Her eyes widened as she studied him, nodding hesitantly. "Sure. Um... can you maybe go wait for me at your truck so I can get out? I'll meet you there once I'm dressed."

Flashing her a smile tinged with more relief than he wanted to admit to at her agreement, he nodded. He didn't say anything else, just stood up and strode toward his truck, leaning against the passenger side with his hands tucked in his pockets.

He still didn't know what the hell he was doing—but he was coming around to the fact that whatever it was, he liked it. He wanted to spend time with her, wanted to get to know her better. Wanted to know everything about her—her secrets, her desires, her wants. What made her tick.

What made her *her*.

And then... maybe he could kiss her again and feel that amazing, soul searing pleasure he felt the first time. He'd been in shock after their first kiss, driving home in a daze that lasted until he fell asleep.

Maybe that was why he felt this need to see her again. He couldn't remember the last time a kiss turned him inside out and made him feel like that.

Hell, who was he trying to kid? No kiss had *ever* done that to him.

Julie had done a number on him, and after they divorced, he'd had no interest in dating or even in women, period. He hadn't wanted to fall into the same trap again. He'd had Mackenzie to take care of, too. He was too busy to get involved with another woman.

He'd tried to convince himself that he couldn't trust Payton. That he knew better than to get involved, and hadn't he learned his lesson the first time? But Payton was nothing like his ex, he knew that with a certainty, and he never could convince himself to be wary of her like that.

So, there he was, as anxious, nervous, and excited to take Payton to dinner as he'd been when he went on his first date in high school.

The sound of footsteps hit his ears and he turned his head, breath catching as he watched Payton walking toward him. She was beyond gorgeous, her long hair pulled up in a ponytail, the damp strands a darker blonde while still wet.

His eyes slid down her body and his lips quirked when he read her shirt. It was black with green writing, and it said *Get Some Tail*, the L on the end turning into a mermaid tail. How many of those shirts did she have? And were *all* of them suggestive?

He'd never thought he was easily manipulated, but in that moment, he wanted to do exactly as her shirt suggested—but only with her.

Tearing his eyes from the letters—and, he couldn't lie, from her chest, seeing as where those letters were placed drew his eyes there like a magnet—he looked at her face, watching as she smiled shyly. He didn't think he'd ever seen her shy, not about anything. And he had to say, he kinda liked it.

Pushing off the truck, he opened her door for her. She took his hand as she climbed in and his heart went crazy, jerking in his chest as his skin tightened.

He didn't think he'd ever get over what the simple act of touching her hand made him feel.

After he got in, he started the truck and then looked over at her. "Do burgers sound okay to you?"

"Yeah, that sounds good."

Nodding, he pulled out onto the main road as they fell

silent. He wasn't feeling shy like she was, exactly, but he was struggling with what to say. It'd been years since he spent time with a woman like this, and nearly as long since he wanted to speak without being his usual surly self.

By the time they pulled up at Burgers AF, they still hadn't spoken. Irritated with himself, he suppressed his sigh as he got out. Before he could open her door, she'd already hopped out, and they walked into the restaurant in silence.

Shit, this was awkward. He needed to cut this shit out and just fucking talk, for crying out loud. Inhaling deeply as he held the door for her and followed her in, he looked around as they walked to the counter.

Burgers AF was one of those unique places that just screamed Aurora Falls to him. Its name was actually Burgers Aurora Falls but he always thought of it as Burgers As Fuck in his head. He glanced at Payton as the cashier came up to take their orders. She placed hers for a Dude, and he ordered a Double Dude before paying and leading her to a table while they waited for their orders to be made.

The names of the different food offerings always made him smile, and he still was as he looked over at her, although it faded as the tension between them made itself known again. Clearing his throat, he leaned in, his eyes intent on her face.

"This feels awkward, doesn't it?"

Her lips curled up in a smile that was tinged with sheepishness and relief—the last probably because he'd finally broken the silence between them.

"A little, yeah. I think we're just not used to interacting with each other like this," she replied, her hand waving between them and the restaurant.

He huffed a laugh. "I'm not really used to interacting with women like this period. At least, not anymore."

Her eyebrows rose. "What do you mean? Are you saying you don't date? Not that I think this is a date or anything," she added hastily, a light blush staining her cheeks.

Suppressing a smile and the chuckle that went with it, he nodded. "Yeah. Julie kind of killed any interest in women. She changed so much after we married, and I was convinced for a long time that all women were like that. Unfair, maybe, but the truth. And then Kenzie got sick, and after her... well, you know how I was. And Payton, for the record... this feels a lot like a date to me."

Her blush deepened but she ignored the part about them being on a date. "She changed a lot after you married?"

"Hold that thought," he said as they called his name for the order. He was back quickly, handing her portion to her and then setting his in front of himself before moving the tray. "The Julie I met was sweet and kind. She went out of her way for everyone. We had a whirlwind courtship and got married a few months later. Eric warned me... he said he could see through her and that the Julie she pretended to be was all an act. I was mad at him for that, but then she showed who she truly was as soon as we were legally bound to each other.

"She let her true colors shine then. The real Julie was a vain, selfish bitch who only cared about herself. Everyone was beneath her in her eyes, and she never hesitated to let people know that. I don't know if you knew this, but the architectural firm I worked for was very successful. I made good money, and that's what she was interested in. It was never about me or falling in love with me—it was about my money and wanting the kind of lifestyle I could give her."

"She was a damned idiot," Payton replied softly. "You're

a good man, Gabe. I could see that even when you were snapping at everyone. If she was more interested in your money than you, she doesn't have the sense God gave a gnat."

He swallowed his bite and chuckled softly. "She was definitely an idiot, but I never thought so because of myself. I thought so because she couldn't ever see past her own self to realize how amazing and beautiful Mackenzie was. She missed out on so much with our daughter and she never even realized it."

Payton shook her head, her sky-blue eyes full of emotion. "I'll never understand that. If I'm ever blessed with children, I'll hold on tightly and never stop loving them. I can't imagine loving myself more than I love them."

"You're so different from her. I think I knew it from the start, but I wouldn't let myself acknowledge it for the longest time. You're the only woman since her who's made me want to open myself up like that again."

She blushed again, smiling shyly as she finished her food. He finished his as well, wondering what to do next. He wasn't ready to take her back to the cabins or to his brother's house, but he wasn't sure what else to suggest.

He was so out of practice with this, and it was painfully obvious.

"My place backs up to the other side of the lake, and the sunset is beautiful from there. You've probably had your fill of the lake, but—"

"I'd love to see the sunset from there," she cut in.

The look on her face made him laugh, although he kept it inside as he nodded and stood up. She looked like she couldn't believe she'd said that and wasn't sure where the words had come from. If he was a different—better—man, he'd give her an out.

But he wasn't, so he didn't. He wanted to spend time with her too much to give her a chance to back out.

They made the drive to his house in silence. Gabe focused on his driving, but the awareness he had of her was off the charts—and he was pretty sure she felt it the same way for him, too. It was mind blowing to him.

All of this was, really. How did he go from not wanting anything to do with her, with any woman, to this? How did he go from being determined to never let on to her that he could see her scale marking—that he might be her mate—to taking her out to dinner and then inviting her back to his place?

He didn't know how to even begin answering that, and before he could try, he was driving down his driveway. Aurora Falls was a small town, so even though he didn't live within the limits, it still took no time at all to get to his house.

Payton gasped and he glanced over to see her staring at his house with wide eyes. "This is your place? Did you design this or was it here when you bought the land?"

Smiling at her obvious pleasure in his home, he hopped out and hurried around the truck before he answered, determined to open the door for her this time. "I designed it. The house I lived in with Julie was pretentious and in an upscale, snobby neighborhood. I hated it from the moment I bought it. Kenzie never liked it, either. She told me she wished we lived in a farmhouse and she described what it looked like in her mind over and over. When I moved here, I decided I'd build the home she wanted. She won't ever get to see it or enjoy it, but it was my small way of honoring her memory. It was the least I could do, since I couldn't bring myself to talk about her until very recently."

CHAPTER 11

Payton's heart clenched at Gabe's words, and she felt an unaccustomed sting of tears in her eyes. Gazing at the farmhouse, she took a moment to control her emotions before she spoke.

"It's a beautiful way to honor her memory," she said softly, still looking at his house. "And I feel like she knows and approves. You guys were living with Eric when it— when she passed, right?"

He nodded, keeping his eyes on the house. "Yeah. She was so sick for so long, and she needed a lot of care. Trying to keep the house and grounds up and give her the care she deserved at the same time was too much for me. I could have hired people to worry about the house for me, but I didn't want strangers tromping through the house when she was so sick and vulnerable."

"I understand that. And like I said, for what it's worth, I think she knows you did this for her. I didn't know her, but I'm sure she loves it."

Clearing his throat gruffly, he nodded again. "Thanks."

He motioned for her to walk to the backyard, and she took a moment to look at the house again before she started walking. It was a large, two story home, with white siding and blue shutters around the windows. There was a big wraparound porch complete with a couple of rocking chairs, and even a porch swing swaying gently in the breeze. An explosion of flowers in every color imaginable spread out along the grass in front of the porch and bracketed the steps.

It was beautiful, but it was a lot of house for one man. She couldn't imagine how lonely it much be for him, rattling around by himself in that large home—especially knowing it was the home of his daughter's dreams, and she'd never gotten to see it.

They walked slowly into the backyard and as the house faded from view, her thoughts turned to what in the world she was doing there with him. When she went into her deep sleep, she'd been resolved to not see him during this moon cycle—yet when she surfaced, he was the first thing she laid eyes on.

She could still barely wrap her mind around the fact that he'd been waiting on her. Even more unbelievable was the fact that he asked her to dinner and then called it a *date*.

Whose life was this? Because it sure as hell didn't feel like hers.

She'd told herself that she needed to keep her distance, so she wasn't sure she should have agreed to any of this. The only reason she could think that she had was because she'd been so stunned by first his appearance, and then him asking her, that she'd just done what she *wanted* without first thinking about doing what she *needed* to do.

Slanting a glance over at him, she had to acknowledge that hanging out with him definitely fell into the *want* category. Butterflies erupted in her belly as he looked over and winked at her, and she hastily turned her attention to the front again. Breath catching, her steps slowed as she caught sight of the lake in front of them.

She'd never seen it from this spot before. The sun was sinking, casting an orange glow onto the calm surface, and she had to admit it was beautiful. That lake had been her prison for a thousand years, but even she could admit, it was gorgeous at times.

Glancing back, she measured the distance between his house and the shore—or at least, she tried to. Distance had never been her thing, but even so, she knew it was pretty close. She could still see the house clearly from the shore.

"I think it's awesome that you have this view from your house."

He nodded, shoving his hands in his pockets. "Yeah. It's part of why I wanted this land. I can't imagine it's such a great view for you, though, seeing as how you live in the lake most of the time. I don't know what I was thinking when I asked if you wanted to come here to see it."

"I have mixed feelings about Sapphire Lake," she replied softly, wrapping her arms around herself. "On one hand, I hate it because I've been chained to it for a century. But I also love it. Hating it for being my prison doesn't mean I can't still see the beauty of it."

"I can't even begin to imagine how it would feel to live like that. I think I would have lost my mind a long time ago."

"You might be surprised. You learn to adapt, learn to live with the hand fate—or a pissed off witch—deals you. It wasn't easy at first, at all, but you have to accept it, or you really will go mad."

Eyebrows twitching, he nodded slowly. "Yeah. It's not the exact same situation, but I know how that feels. Kind of like what I had to do when Mackenzie passed away—although I guess it didn't seem like I dealt with it at all. I did, though, in my own way. I wouldn't be alive right now if I hadn't."

She reached out, touching his arm softly. She honestly didn't know how to reply, but she decided to just wing it. "That's understandable. I don't know what it's like to lose a child, but it was the same way for me at first. Losing my parents and siblings, losing my very way of life... I wasn't always this accepting and bubbly. It took years and years—at least a hundred, if not more—before I could accept that this is my life now. And maybe just as long before I could find happiness in it again."

She started to pull her hand away, and he reached up, catching it with his own and twining their fingers together. Her heart leaped as his touch sent goosebumps dancing over her skin. The sensation was starting to become familiar, as familiar as the heat licking up her spine.

How did he make her feel so much just from one touch?

"I think we've both had a rough go of it. *Both* of us. Sometimes you sound like you shouldn't have negative feelings about what happened to you, because me or someone else has had it worse—or at least, they have it worse in your eyes. But that's not right, Pay.

"Someone else is *always* gonna have it worse than we do. But that doesn't mean we're not entitled to our feelings. It doesn't make our emotions about what we're going through any less real or valid. If you're feeling something, let yourself. Pushing it to the backburner just because you think you shouldn't feel it isn't going to help you work through it."

Her nose stung with the urge to shed a few tears and she inhaled, trying to beat them back. A moment later, she huffed a laugh, amused at herself. He'd just gotten through telling her to let herself feel her feelings, and her first inclination was to bury her emotions.

But she didn't want to cry in front of him—even though those words had been beautiful to her.

"I do that a lot," she acknowledged softly. "I started doing it as a defense mechanism for my overwhelming emotions after the curse. Things couldn't really be that bad if others had it worse, ya know? But now I feel genuinely bad if I get in my emotions. I can't help it. It's second nature to me now."

"Just try to remember that you're entitled to how you feel, no matter what it's about or what other people have going on in their lives."

She smiled up a him, suddenly feeling shy again. "I will."

His eyes darkened as they dropped to her lips, and her breathing stuttered as his fingers tightened around hers. She'd gone into the deep sleep merfolk could go into this past month, but the last thing she thought of before falling asleep had been his kiss—and it had been the first thing she thought of upon awakening.

He leaned in slowly, clearly giving her time to pull away if she didn't want this. But even though stopping it would be for the best, she couldn't bring herself to. She wanted to feel the magic of his kiss again too badly.

She wanted this. She wanted *him*.

When his lips touched hers, it was like her soul sighed with relief. He kept it gentle for about two seconds and then he roughly pulled her into him, wrapping his arms around her as he deepened the kiss. Knees weakening, she twined her arms around his neck, giving into him, the kiss, and the heat blazing its way up her spine.

He slid his tongue along her lips, and she opened to give him entry, one hand running up into his hair as she dug the nails of her other into his shoulder. He tangled his tongue with hers for several long moments before pulling back and nipping her bottom lip. Her insides felt like they liquified as he soothed the sting with his tongue before slipping it back inside her mouth, and she moaned as his hands slipped down, palming her ass and bringing her in closer.

He was already hard, his length pressing against her, and she couldn't help arching her back, rubbing herself against him. Groaning, he pulled her in tighter as his kiss turned uncontrolled, passion blazing between them.

Payton wasn't sure how long they stood there, making out like each other's lips were the air they needed and they'd die if they stopped, but when he eased back, the sun had nearly sunk in the sky. Their harsh breathing seemed loud in the quiet night, and Gabe pressed his forehead to hers for a moment. He looked like he was struggling to find the right words, and when he eased away and met her eyes, the heat in his liquid brown depths making her glad she was still holding onto him.

"Do you want to come inside?" he asked, his voice hesitant and unsure for the first time since she met him. "There's no pressure if you don't want to, sweetheart. And we can go in without going to the bedroom. Dammit, I feel like I'm making a mess of this, and I don't know when I turned into a man who felt like he had to dance around shit—"

Laughing softly, she put her finger on his mouth, halting his rapid-fire speech. "I'd love to go inside. But maybe the tour of the house can wait until after the tour of the bedroom."

Lord, who was she? This wasn't the Payton she'd known for a thousand years—that Payton didn't so brazenly accept an offer to *tour* a man's bedroom. But she had no desire to take the words back. She wanted this too badly. Wanted *him* too badly.

His eyes practically smoldered at her as he smiled slowly—sexily. Reaching down, he took her hand again, twining their fingers together, and led her back to his house at a fast pace. Giggling, she hurried to keep pace with him, watching as he pulled the keys out of his pocket and jiggled them until he found the one for the backdoor.

Pulling her inside, he kicked the door shut behind them and pushed her against the wall, giving her a blistering kiss. She gasped into his mouth as she pressed her body against his, her blood boiling as his hand slid under the hem of her shirt.

The feel of him, skin to skin, made her shudder as desire nearly buckled her knees. He slowly made his way up her ribcage, still kissing the breath right out of her, and she thought she was going to lose her mind if he didn't reach his destination soon.

To her immense frustration, he pulled his hand out of her shirt at the same time he sucked her bottom lip into his mouth. Tugging it gently with his teeth, he eased away, grabbing her hand again and leading her to the front of the house and up the stairs.

Her heart was pounding so hard she was surprised it didn't break right through her ribcage, but it wasn't because they were practically racing up the stairs. It was because of what he'd already made her feel, what she knew he was *going* to make her feel.

He told her to feel her emotions, and she was going to revel in the way she felt in that moment. She didn't think she'd ever in her life—even when she stood at the prow of the old ships a thousand years ago—felt anything this amazing, this exhilarating.

Gabe pulled her into what she assumed was his bedroom. She honestly wasn't sure, because she didn't take any time to look around. Feeling bold, her shyness with him completely gone in that moment, she reached down, grabbed the hem of her shirt, and pulled it over her head.

He sucked in a quick breath as his eyes dropped to take her in, but she didn't give him time, immediately grabbing his shirt and tugging it up. Taking the hint, he pulled it off, and her breath caught. This time, she let him have his moment to stare at her, because all she wanted to do was drink him in.

Sweet heavens, he was gorgeous. His shoulders and chest were broad, his large pecs leading down to chiseled abs she wanted to trace with her tongue. His torso narrowed to the V of his hips, and a happy trail led down from his belly button, disappearing beneath the waistband of his jeans.

Swallowing hard, she raised her eyes just as he did the same, and then they lunged for each other. He kissed her deeply, one hand pulling her ponytail holder out and then tangling in the hair at the back of her head. It felt like he was trying to devour her, and between that and the way he felt pressed against her, skin to skin, his hardness digging into her belly, she was done. A goner. Completely and totally his, a slave to the sensations burning through her and the way he made her feel.

His hand in her hair tightened and he pulled her head back as he broke the kiss. He pressed his lips to the skin just under her chin and slid them down, licking and nipping as he slowly kissed his way down.

Reaching her collarbone, he traced its length with his tongue before moving down, ever so slowly dragging it down her cleavage. Moaning, she pushed in tighter against him, wishing her bra would just magically disappear.

Like he was reading her mind, he let her hair go and reached behind her. His fingers fumbled with the clasp for a moment before he got it unhooked, and the reminder that he hadn't done this in a long time sent a wave of warmth through her that had nothing to do with the desire overwhelming her senses.

Easing back, he put his fingertips on the straps, slowly pulling the bra off her arms and letting it drop to the floor. His quiet groan echoed through the room as he clenched his jaw, shaking his head back and forth.

"You're so fucking gorgeous," he said hoarsely as he met her eyes. The grittiness in his voice made her stomach clench deliciously and she swallowed hard as a fresh wave of heat washed over her.

"You're not so bad yourself."

She tried her damnedest to speak in a normal voice, but all she could manage was a whisper that was shaky with desire. A corner of his mouth lifted, showing off the groove in his cheek, and he pulled her into him again. She gasped as she finally felt him with no clothes between their upper bodies, and when he pulled back and his hand started the journey from her waist to her breast, she literally trembled with desire.

This time, he didn't stop until he reached his destination, and her eyes rolled back in her head as he kneaded her breast gently. His other hand cupped her other breast and she gasped, moisture flooding her core, as his thumbs began playing with her nipples.

Leaning over, he trailed his mouth down her chest again, not pausing until he had his mouth wrapped around her nipple. As he sucked, flicking it with his tongue, his fingers mimicked the motion on her other nipple.

Payton felt lightheaded and she sucked in a breath, not realizing until that moment that she hadn't been breathing. Head falling back, she gripped his shoulders tightly, trying with the last shred of awareness she had to not dig her fingernails in too hard.

Letting her nipple slip from his mouth with a pop, he made his way over to the other one, repeating the process all over again. He was stealing all her wits with his mouth, but she retained just enough to finally become an active participant.

She loved the way he was making her feel, but she wanted to touch him, too. No, it wasn't just a want, it was a *need*, and she was helpless to resist the pull. Finally loosening her grip, she slowly slid her hands down his chest. She couldn't go far because he was still sucking her nipples for all he was worth, but it was enough.

Between the feel of his pecs under her hands and the way his mouth was making her crazy with yearning and desire, it was a wonder she wasn't a puddle at his feet. He was pulling reactions from her that she never even knew she was capable of.

He pulled away, capturing her mouth hungrily, and she moaned, reveling in the fact that she could finally touch him more thoroughly. She ran her fingers over his abs, exploring to her heart's content before moving on to the V that made her stupid when she saw it, thinking to herself that she needed to retrace the same route with her tongue when it wasn't so busy dueling with his.

Her fingers got to his waistband and she couldn't stop her smile when he sucked in a breath, his abs quivering. But before she could dip her fingers inside, he broke the kiss and went after her own jeans, unbuttoning and unzipping them so fast it made her head spin.

He yanked them down, urging her to step out of them, and the moment she did, he hooked his arms around her thighs and picked her up. Giggling breathlessly as a surge of pure need shot through her, she wrapped her legs around his waist, gasping as her center rubbed against the hardness straining his jeans.

Gabe let out a deep groan that vibrated through his chest, and she felt it down to her core as he whipped them around and walked toward the bed. Putting an arm out, he lowered her and then straightened back up, gazing at her with so much heat that she felt it brushing down her skin.

He leaned down again, bracing himself on one arm, his muscles bulging, as he took her hand and held it against his heart. "Feel that, Payton? Do you feel what you do to me? My heart is going to beat right out of my chest."

Her own heart jumped and then melted as she felt his pounding under her fingers. Easing away, he took a few steps away from the bed, his hands going to the button of his jeans. Mouth instantly drying, she swallowed hard, scooting up the bed until she was by the pillows, propping herself up on her elbows so she could see him better.

Flashing a devilish smile that damned near melted her panties, he popped the button and eased the zipper down slowly, hissing out a breath as he worked it past his erection. In one fluid movement, he pushed his jeans down, stepping out of them and straightening back up.

Her breath caught as the flames licking up her spine burned hotter. She didn't think she'd ever seen a man who looked like him in person. He was tall, thick with muscle, his hard erection standing up straight and proud, with a drop of moisture on the tip.

Swallowing hard, she couldn't help but gaze at it for a moment. Long and thick, it had veins running the length, and an angry, purple head that was practically begging for release. Blowing out a breath as her core clenched deliciously at the thought of having it inside her, she finally dragged her gaze away, taking all of him in again.

Whether what they were doing was right or wrong, whether it actually should be happening or not—she knew she'd remember this moment forever. When she was spending her mandatory month in the lake, she'd pull this moment out and replay it over and over.

The thought made her sad, so she forced her thoughts away as she met his gaze, nearly whimpering at the look in the liquid brown depths. It was intense, hot, full of the promise that he was going to eat her up—and that she'd enjoy every moment.

Prowling forward, he climbed onto the bed and crawled over her. Her legs fell open without conscious thought as he settled himself between them, holding himself up on his arms. Leaning down, he devoured her mouth, swallowing her gasp as he kissed her hungrily.

But it didn't last long. Leaving her lips, he trailed his mouth down her neck, stopping at her breasts again, while his hand continued on. He sucked her nipple in his mouth at the same time he slipped his hand into her panties, running his finger over her folds, collecting the wetness there.

"Fuck, you're so wet," he growled against her breast, making her arch her back as it vibrated straight through her.

All she could manage as a reply was a garbled noise as his fingers slipped inside her. He circled her clit a few times, never quite touching directly on it, making her let out a noise of frustration as she fisted the sheets in her hands.

"Patience, baby."

His endearment in that hoarse, gritty voice damned near did her in. Moving his fingers, he slipped one inside her before adding a second as he tongued her nipple, and her core clenched as she arched into his touch.

She was already on the edge, so close to what she knew would be an epic orgasm. It wouldn't take much, but he seemed content to just tease her, moving his fingers in and out of her slowly as he lightly ran his tongue over her nipple.

Just as her frustration got the better of her and she opened her mouth to order him to do more, he pulled his fingers out of her and swirled them around her clit again. He moved them faster and faster, closing the circle with every pass, and right before she squeezed her eyes shut, she saw him press his hips into the bed, like he needed the pressure himself.

Satisfaction filled her that he was torturing himself just as much as he was her. It was her last coherent thought as he *finally* rubbed directly over her swollen nub. A few passes were all it took, her body already strung so tightly she thought she was going to shatter.

He pressed down, rubbing firmly directly over her nub at the same time that he lightly bit her nipple—and she flew and shattered at the same time. That was what it felt like. Like she shattered completely apart, and then all the broken pieces that made her who she was flew up in the air.

And an eternity later, when all the pieces floated to the ground and put themselves back together, they didn't form the same person. She was completely different, and she honestly didn't know if she liked the new her or not.

She'd need time to get to know her, that was for sure.

Gabe distracted her from her admittedly crazy

thoughts, surging up to kiss her hungrily. He somehow managed to hook his thumbs in her panties and pull them down, but he could only go so far without breaking the kiss.

He growled against her lips and she smiled against his, reaching down to help him take them off. Flinging them across the room somewhere, he settled between her legs and she gasped as his hot erection pressed against her center.

A moment later, he cursed as he surged up to his knees, looking around the room wildly before he lunged over to open the bedside drawer. He pulled out a condom with a triumphant smile that faded as he studied it.

"I honestly don't know how old this is," he said, his voice still gritty and raw. "There's a good chance it's *way* too old. Fuckin' hell."

Biting her lip, she looked from him to the condom and back again. She didn't want to stop what they were doing, and she knew he didn't either. She wasn't worried about diseases—she didn't have any, and judging by how long it'd been for him, he didn't either.

"I'm clean. And it's the wrong time for a pregnancy. The odds are basically nonexistent. So, if you use it and it fails for whatever reason, everything will still be good. I still want this. I hope you do, too."

His eyes darkened as he stared at her and then with a soft curse, he tore the wrapper open with shaky fingers. "Fuck yes, I do. I'm clean, too. And I'm sure it'll hold up fine. I've bought some over the years, I just can't remember when I bought this one. I'm sure it'll be fine."

She smiled, relief washing over her that he wasn't going to stop. He wasn't her mate—and she had to force away the sadness that rose up inside her at the thought—and she'd be the first person to put a halt to this if she thought it could lead to repercussions neither one was ready for.

Besides, until the curse was broken, she couldn't get pregnant. But she didn't want to bring that up or even think about it in that moment. For once, she wanted to just be a woman, one who was about to be loved senseless by a sexy man—not a cursed mermaid who didn't function as a normal woman would.

Heat flared inside her anew as she watched him roll the condom over his impressive erection, and she smiled as he fell back over her, his weight propped up on his arms as he kissed her. This time, when his dick brushed her folds, she arched her back, following it with her hips.

She was beyond ready to have him inside her. Honestly, she thought she wanted it just as much as she wanted to be free of the curse, and the thought completely freaked her out.

Before she could get worked up over it, he reached down, taking himself in hand and rubbing his dick through her folds, deliberately bumping her clit with ever pass. She let out a moan before her breath caught, pleasure streaking through her nerve endings every time he rubbed her swollen nub.

He finally positioned himself at her entrance and she rolled her eyes closed as he slowly pushed inside her. She felt herself stretching to accommodate him, and she was glad he was easing his way in. It'd been a long time for her—about a thousand years, give or take a few years—and he wasn't exactly a small man.

Despite the stretch, pleasure lit up her nerve endings as another wave of heat washed over her. Honestly, even the stretch felt good to her—and then, with a surge of his hips, he buried himself to the hilt inside her, and she was no longer capable of rational thought.

Digging her fingers into his back, not able to bring

herself to worry about whether she was drawing blood or not, she let out a moan at the same time he groaned. He pressed his forehead against hers, not moving yet, his arms trembling on either side of her head.

Whether that was from the strain of holding himself up or from the desire she could see burning in his liquid brown eyes, she wasn't sure.

Ever so slowly, he pulled almost all the way out of her and then pushed back inside, and she gasped as pleasure washed over her. He did that over and over, speeding up just a tiny bit every time he pulled out, until he was rocking into her powerfully.

Wrapping her legs around his waist, she moved in time with him, raising her hips to meet his thrusts, eyes squeezed shut so tightly that she saw stars. His hips sped up, the sound of them slapping into hers echoing through the room, as his rhythm faltered. A moment later, he was slamming into her, all of his finesse gone as he pounded his hips.

And she *loved* it.

Rearing back, he hooked an arm around her waist, holding her up as he moved in and out of her. It changed the angle of his thrusts, and pleasure washed over in even stronger waves than before. Reaching down, he placed his thumb on her clit, rubbing in time with his thrusts, and that was all it took.

If she thought she shattered apart before, it was nothing compared to how she felt this time. She burst apart from the pleasure as she soared, fighting and failing to suck in a breath as her orgasm overwhelmed her.

She was vaguely aware of Gabe cursing, his hips stuttering as he followed her. She could feel him pulsing inside of her, and it made the pleasure she felt intensify to the point where she thought she couldn't possibly withstand it.

Eventually, she floated back down, blinking her eyes as she felt like she was finally herself again. Gabe was pulling out of her gently, and he winked at her as he left the bed, heading to what she assumed was the bathroom to dispose of the condom.

Her body was limp, and her limbs felt like overcooked noodles. She had no strength to move, and her eyelids grew heavy as she waited for him to return. That had been... well, she didn't have words for it, but she knew she wasn't the same after.

He came back in and laid on the bed, immediately pulling her into his arms. She snuggled in, her body sated, her heart content, the aftershocks of pleasure still washing over her.

Agreeing to go with him to dinner was one of the best decisions she'd ever made.

CHAPTER 12

GABE RAN HIS FINGERTIPS GENTLY UP AND DOWN Payton's arm, his mind racing. He was exhausted, but his thoughts hadn't slowed for even a second, and he knew he wouldn't be able to fall asleep any time soon.

He'd never expected to feel so much for her. And it wasn't just about the sex—although holy hell, he never imagined making love to her would feel like that. Like she was everything he always wanted but never thought actually existed.

But it was more than that. He could feel his heart softening toward her. Hell, he was sure it'd been doing that since they met. And even though he tried to harden it, tried to keep his wall between them up, he couldn't manage it.

His walls crumbled to dust when she was around, and no amount of hastily applied patchwork could fix them.

He'd been telling her the truth earlier—she was nothing like Julie. The way he felt for her scared him, though. He was man enough to admit that. They might have known each other for a while now, but he hadn't allowed himself to get close to her—and apparently, she'd been avoiding him because he'd still been lost in his grumpy, surly daze.

When Ariel got sick—that was when they really started to get to know each other. Which meant that the swiftness his feelings for her came to be was terrifying to a man like him.

No, she wasn't his ex-wife, and he was reminded of that every time he looked into her eyes and every time they talked. But he couldn't help being worried that he'd be fooled again and end up in a situation like his marriage.

Only what she wanted wouldn't be his money—it would be freedom from the curse she was under.

His thoughts made him feel like even more of a dick than he normally felt. He knew she desperately wanted free from the curse, but he also knew she'd never think to use him—or any man—to break it. She didn't even know they were mates, and the guilt he felt from keeping that from her was damned near choking him.

Suppressing a sigh, he glanced down at her and then pressed a kiss to her light blonde hair. He was going to tell her. He never should have tried to keep it from her to begin with, and he damned sure couldn't now. Not after what they'd shared.

Even though he felt like he could go all in with her in this very moment, he wasn't sure it was the best idea. Maybe they needed a little more time together—although his heart was telling him they didn't need more time; it was already all in with her. But that didn't mean he had to keep the truth from her any longer.

She deserved to know.

And there was the not so small fact that he knew, if she found out before he could tell her, it could completely wreck what they were building together. He might have been on the fence about whether he wanted this with her up until that morning, but he already couldn't stand the thought that she might not want a place in his life.

A yawn broke through and he closed his eyes, tightening his arm around her. He'd tell her in the morning and pray for the best.

Because he couldn't imagine a life without her now. Putting his faith in a woman still scared him, but not half as much as living without her did.

CHAPTER 13

THE PRESSING NEED TO USE THE BATHROOM PULLED AT Payton's consciousness. She tried to beat it back, not wanting to leave her comfy spot in the covers, but it eventually forced her to open her eyes.

The first thing she saw was the heavy, masculine arm wrapped around her waist, and she smiled as memories of the night before flooded her. She'd never imagined it could be like that between them—hell, she hadn't thought it could be like that period, with any man.

She literally tingled from the memories, and she felt her heart warm as she tried to slip out from under Gabe's arm and he tightened it in response. She desperately wanted to snuggle back in with him, but she really needed to relieve her bladder first.

Quickly finishing, she washed her hands and walked back into the bedroom, pausing in front of the bed as she took Gabe in. He was still asleep, one arm stretched out where she'd been, like he was still reaching for her.

His hair was in a mess around his head, and the covers were pooled around his waist, showing off his gorgeous torso. Her heart literally ached as she looked at him and she had to face the facts—she was falling in love with him.

Hell, maybe she was already there.

It felt like it happened so fast, her head was spinning from it. From avoiding him at all costs just a month before to loving him that quickly... But maybe it had always been there. She'd been insanely attracted to him at first, but his general jerkiness had kept her from wanting to get to know the man beneath the handsome exterior.

But maybe she hadn't been as opposed to him as she thought she was. Even though she tried to avoid him, she knew why he acted the way he did. It was possible that she'd let her emotions stay involved with him even when she tried to avoid him, because she knew that who he was on the exterior wasn't who he was on the interior.

It didn't matter how or why, though. It only mattered that she was falling in love with him now. And if he thought he could make it work with a mermaid who was sentenced to live most of her life in the lake, well, she was willing to give it a shot, too.

Even though she was almost positive that it would end in heartbreak for one of them—most likely her. Because how could she possibly expect a man like him to be okay with having a lover he could only see for roughly three days a month?

The answer was simple. She couldn't.

So, it would end one day, probably sooner rather than later, and then she'd be left with a broken heart. But she couldn't bring herself to care about that in that moment. She'd bask in every second they were together, and she'd love him for all she was worth—and when he wanted to move on, she'd let him go without making him feel like he had any obligation to her.

The thought made her heart hurt and she reached up to rub her chest. But as she stared at him, she became aware of a ball of energy in her chest. Frowning, she puzzled over it, wondering what the hell it was—and then it hit her.

It was a mating bond.

And she was feeling it for Gabe.

Intense joy filled her, so much that she was hardly able to breathe through it. Her fears just a moment ago were unfounded, then. They wouldn't be forced to live a half relationship, only able to see each other during the cycle of the full moon. They could have a real, honest to God relationship, because once the bond was fully formed, it would break the curse and she'd be free of her lake prison.

Gabe was her mate. How had she gotten so lucky? The odds of that happening were pretty much slim to none, and yet there was no denying the bond she felt in her soul. He shifted on the bed, and her smile was instantaneous when she saw the scale marking on his arm, in the same spot hers was in. It just confirmed what she'd already known.

They were mates.

A moment later, her smile faltered, a frown taking its place. She glanced from his new mark to her own as her blood turned cold and dread welled up inside her. She tried to slow her emotions down, to reason her way through it, but it was no use.

Because there was no way he hadn't already known they were mates. He'd probably known from the very beginning—from the moment he learned about mermaids and the curse, at the very least.

Her mark was in an obvious spot. There was no way in hell he could have missed it. Not to mention, he'd touched every inch of her last night. And when a mate touched the mark for the first time, the clan's history played out before them. He'd never once looked like he was learning her history the night before, and he sure as hell never mentioned it.

Pain lanced through her chest and she sucked in a breath of air. Her mind flashed back to the moment the month before when she stumbled in the woods and he grabbed her arm—right over the scales. She thought then that something had stunned him, but when he said he was just worried she'd hurt herself, she accepted it and never gave it another thought.

But now she knew he'd been seeing her history, and that was what had him looking so stunned.

Tears welled up in her eyes as she drew in a hitching breath, tracing trembling fingers over her mark. He'd known at least that long, but it had to be longer. There was no way an observant man like him would miss her obvious mark for that long.

Was the night before all about getting laid? She'd thought they were developing an important emotional connection, but now she thought, for him at least, it had all been about getting some. What else could it be about, after all? He'd known they were mates, that they had something life changing and amazing, and he hadn't let on about it even once.

Her tears cleared as anger rose up inside her. It wasn't over the fact that he hadn't told her, although that was part of it—it was over the fact that he'd used her to slake his physical needs.

Used her.

The words were ugly and she hated them, but they were maybe the most accurate words she'd ever thought.

Inhaling deeply, she tore her gaze from him, looking around for her panties. She didn't see them, but she could just put her jeans on without them. She didn't need them that badly.

Stalking over to where they were thrown on the floor, she bent to pick them up, freezing when she heard the sheets rustling on the bed. She didn't want to look at him, and she hoped he wasn't waking up, because she didn't want to talk to him, either.

A hope that was blown all to hell when he spoke. "Payton? What are you doing? Come back to bed."

She felt the sting of tears against her eyelids again, and she dashed a hand over them before she faced him, pissed that he was making her feel the hurt all over again. She much preferred anger over this soul searing pain.

"You knew," she whispered shakily, trying to give her voice more substance without making her pain obvious to him.

Frowning, he sat up on the bed, his eyes sleepy. "What?"

Clearing her throat and willing steel into her spine that she didn't feel, she pointed at his arm. "You knew we were mates and you didn't say a word. Was last night all about getting laid? Fucking me was more important than telling me the truth?"

Flinching at her words, he glanced down at his arm, paling when he saw the scale marking on his arm. He looked back up at her, his brown eyes wide and panicked. "Pay, no. You've got it all wrong. Let me explain."

"The time for explanations passed a long time ago. Back when you first saw my mark, maybe, but even if you didn't want to be my mate, I at least deserved to know the truth before we slept together."

"You're right, but—"

Not wanting to hear what his *but* might be, she threw

down her jeans and turned toward the door. "Screw your explanations and screw my clothes. I don't need them, anyway."

"Payton, wait!"

But she didn't pause. Instead, she put on a burst of speed as she went down the stairs and out the back door. Gabe didn't have any neighbors, so she didn't have to worry about anyone seeing her running naked across his lawn, and she didn't need her clothes where she was going.

She might not know her way around this side of the lake on land, but she knew every inch of the lake under the surface.

And for the first time since she was cursed, she jumped into the lake long before her three days were up—where she just might stay for the next hundred years or so.

CHAPTER 14

GABE CURSED LOUDLY, YANKING HIS HAND THROUGH his hair as he paced in front of the lake. Why had he bothered to put his clothes on? It took precious time he hadn't been able to afford, and his land was remote enough that he had no neighbors who could see—something Payton obviously figured out for herself, since she took off naked like a bat out of hell.

He burst outside just in time to see her diving into the lake—the one place he couldn't follow her.

Turning, he made his way back inside, anger and desperation burning through him. The anger wasn't directed at Payton... it was directed solely at himself. He never should have let things get as far as they had without telling her the truth.

It was a monumental fuck up, and he only had himself to blame.

The desperation was one hundred percent for her, though. He had to figure out how to win her back, but how could he do that if she hid out in the lake? His heart literally hurt at the thought that he might not ever see her again, let alone make her understand.

He got to the top of the stairs, intent on going to his room and showering while he tried to figure out his next move. Walking into his room, his eyes fell on her clothes on the floor, and he bent to pick them up, unable to handle seeing them lie forgotten on the floor.

Folding them quickly, he set them on the dresser, his eyes catching on the scale marking on his arm. Swallowing hard, he traced it with his fingers, his heart clenching. He should have told her sooner. He should have told her the moment he saw it, but he damned sure should have said something before they made love.

He stood a chance of her understanding why he held his silence before that, but now it looked like exactly what she said—that all he'd wanted was to get his dick wet.

He had to figure out how to win her back. He loved her, and he couldn't live without her.

Pausing as he started to step in the shower, he went over the words in his mind, testing them, seeing how much truth there was in them. But he couldn't find any holes anywhere in the thought.

He loved her. So fucking much. And he *needed* her in his life. If he had to put on scuba gear and find her in the lake, he would. It would make it difficult to talk, but he'd find a way around that.

He had to. Payton was his life, and he wasn't letting her walk away from him without a fight.

Twenty minutes later, he was out of the shower and dressed, in his truck heading to Eric and Ailani's. He was going to exhaust all his options and asking Ailani to talk to her friend was one of them. But he hadn't been kidding about the scuba gear—he'd do that if he had to.

Inhaling deeply, he knocked on the door, waiting for someone to answer it. A few minutes passed by before Eric opened the door, eyebrows raising as he saw him there.

"Gabe, we weren't expecting you. Come on in."

Following him to the living room, he tried again to figure out what to say or where to start, but he still hadn't come up with anything by the time they were all sitting. His brother and sister-in-law stared at him expectantly and he cleared his throat, searching for words.

"I did something stupid," he said, studying his linked fingers. "I totally screwed up, and I'm not sure Payton will ever forgive me."

Eric frowned at him, but it was Ailani who spoke first. "This is about Payton? What happened?"

"I'm Payton's mate—"

Ailani's gasp cut him off. "You are? That's wonderful! See, Eric, I told you months ago I thought they might be mates."

Eric reached out, putting his hand over his mate's and squeezing. "Let's not get too excited just yet. He already said he screwed it up."

She frowned as she looked over at him. "That's right. What happened?"

Shit, he didn't want to tell her. Ailani was tiny, but she had a temper that matched her fiery red hair, and the last thing he wanted to do was tell her he fucked up and broke her best friend's heart.

But the whole reason he came here was to try to get her help, so he was going to suck it up, find his balls, and tell her the truth.

"I knew that I was her mate the first time I met her, because you'd already told me about mermaids, the markings, the curse, and mates. But I wasn't ready for her. I honestly didn't think I'd ever be ready for her, and I thought she was better off without me. I thought there had to be another mate out there for her who wasn't as emotionally damaged as I was—as I am."

"There's only one true mate for each of us," Ailani broke in, her frown growing. "Only one person who can break the curse."

He shrugged helplessly. "I didn't know that. But we started growing closer when Ariel was sick... and when she came back to the surface yesterday, I was waiting for her. I couldn't stay away, and until she showed up, I still didn't think it meant what it did. But when she got there, I asked her to dinner, and I realized after that that it wasn't the nothing I thought it was. I realized I loved her. And then we —well, she slept at my house last night. I was going to tell her the truth this morning but before I could, she saw the mark on my arm and realized we were mates. And before I could explain, she took off and went back into the lake."

Eric's frown turned into a scowl. "You mean you slept with her without telling her you were mates, and she found out on her own and ditched your ass? I don't blame her for going back into the lake. I would have, too."

Ailani shook her head as she cut her husband a look. "Stop. That's not going to help anything." She went quiet for a moment, biting her lip as she studied Gabe. "I can't say I'm not disappointed. You should have told her before things got that far between you. I can understand why she's hurt, but I also understand your side of things. Julie's behavior scarred you, and then after Mackenzie passed away, you gave up on the world and everyone in it. I know it takes time to move past stuff like that—but I wish you'd talked to Pay before you became intimate."

"Trust me, so do I. I've been feeling guilty about not telling her what we were to each other ever since the weekend with Ariel. But it wasn't until I saw her again yesterday that I realized I began falling in love with her that weekend. I know I should have told her everything then, but things went so fast last night, and all I was thinking about was keeping her close. But I know I screwed up royally by not telling her then."

"I'm not judging you, Gabe. I was the one pushing Eric away when we met. I was terrified of getting my heart broken and I refused to believe that the curse could be broken by finding my mate. I fought him with everything in me, and I put off telling him the truth about myself for so long that I was forced into the lake before I could tell him everything.

"Like I said, I'm not judging you—but you better make it all good with my best friend. Payton's the one who got me through the last thousand years with any shred of my sanity intact. She's been longing for her mate since the moment we were cursed—before that, even, because all she's ever wanted was a family—and she never lets her optimism flag. She pulled me kicking and screaming out of my depression, and I hate the thought of her being hurt or feeling that depression herself in any way."

Swallowing hard, he nodded, her words making the shame he'd been trying to beat back wash over him like a tidal wave. Honestly, though, he deserved to feel every bit of it and more for letting things with him and Payton even get to this point.

"I understand. And I'll spend the rest of my life making this up to her, if she'll let me."

Ailani smiled at him. "I know you will. How can we help you? I'm assuming you're telling us this because you need our help."

Gabe nodded. "We'll do whatever we can. You fucked up big on this one, but we love both you and Payton, and we want you guys to be happy."

He cleared his throat, feeling an unaccustomed surge of

emotion. He had amazing people in his life, but he'd pushed them all away after Mackenzie died. He should have leaned on them, Eric especially since he hadn't known Ailani then, and let them help him through it.

If he had, he might not be here, having to plead for help to win his mate back. He would have accepted what she was to him a long time ago, and he wouldn't be in this position now.

He never would have broken Payton's heart—and he knew he had. He'd seen the look in her eyes when she confronted him this morning. It was a look that would haunt him until the end of his days, even if he could win her back.

No—there was no *could* about it. He *had* to get her back. Life meant nothing without her.

Blowing out a breath, he forced his emotions down as he looked up at them. "Payton went back in the lake before I had a chance to explain. I thought about getting some scuba gear and diving in after her, but that would mean I still couldn't talk to her. So, I was hoping..."

He let his words trail off and Ailani instantly nodded. "You need me to go talk to her. Too easy. Let me get my shoes on and I'll walk to the lake and go in. I'll do my best to get her to come up to the surface, but she might need some time, Gabe. Payton's emotions have always been strong, and she might be too hurt to come back up right away."

"As long as someone talks to her, I'm happy. I don't want her to keep thinking all I wanted from her was sex. That had nothing to do with it. As long as she knows that, I can wait for as long as I need to." He hoped, anyway.

Eric smirked. "I'm pretty sure sex had at least a little to do with it."

Ailani frowned at her mate before looking back at him

with gentle moss green eyes. "I'll make sure I tell her that part, too."

"I'll drive you," Eric said, standing when she did. "I don't want you walking when you don't have to."

"Fine, but you really need to give me more driving lessons. It would be easier on all of us if I could drive myself where I need to go."

She walked out of the room and Eric shuddered as he looked at Gabe. "Her driving is horrible. Can you see the grey in my hair yet? I swear I get more every time she gets behind the wheel."

He huffed a laugh, a tiny spark of amusement flaring inside him before it quickly died. "She's right, though. It would be easier if she could drive."

Eric nodded, his pale green eyes serious as he looked at him. "I know. Look, I really hope everything works out between you two. You've been acting more alive in this past month than I've seen you in years, and I want to keep seeing you like this. You deserve happiness, Gabe. I better go get my shoes on and get Ariel ready before Lani takes off on her own, but can I give you a bit of advice for when you see Payton again?"

"Of course. I'll take all the advice I can get."

"Let me see your phone."

Brow twitching, he reached into his pocket and pulled it out, handing it to his brother. Eric fiddled around on it for a moment and then handed it back with amusement in his eyes.

"I'm gonna give you the same advice Ailani's brother gave me when I first met her. Play that, then get your ass home and play it again until it really sinks in. And never stop doing what it says, for as long as you live, and maybe you might be able to hold onto a woman like Payton."

He frowned, watching as Eric shoved his feet into his shoes and jogged over to where Ailani was carrying Ariel. He took the baby from her and led her out, and Gabe finally looked down at his phone as the door closed behind them, a smile that was half amused and half bittersweet stretching his lips when he saw the song his brother pulled up on YouTube.

Pushing play, he sat back in his chair as the beginning strains of "Kiss the Girl" from Disney's The Little Mermaid filled the air. He hadn't known Tai told Eric to do this when they first met, although he'd of course known the Disney movie was a huge joke between them.

The Little Mermaid had been his daughter's favorite movie, and it was probably crazy, but as he listened to the song, it felt like Mackenzie was blessing the fact that Payton was his. She would have loved her, and he knew Payton would have adored her in return. He only wished they'd gotten the chance to meet each other.

He listened to the whole song play through and then he stood, making his way to his truck. That was one piece of advice from his brother that he was absolutely going to take. He was going to kiss the hell out of the girl when he saw her again—and he refused to even contemplate never laying eyes on her again.

He'd give her time, like Ailani said she might need, but if she didn't come back to the surface on her own, he was going to look into renting that scuba gear.

CHAPTER 15

Payton swam back and forth in the cave, unable to stop moving. When she first got down here, she tried to go into the deep mermaid sleep, but her heart hurt too much to allow her to slip into it, and she quickly gave up.

Her heart might not *ever* stop hurting enough to allow it.

She'd known Gabe was damaged, but she hadn't thought it was so bad that he could use people for his own pleasure.

Use. There was that word again, and with it came the accompanying pain—not that she'd stopped hurting from the moment she realized he knew they were mates. She hadn't, but she obviously had triggers that were going to make the pain worse.

Hopefully, they'd fade with time, but she wasn't holding her breath. For a brief, shining moment in time, she'd loved him with everything in her. Maybe they hadn't been close for a long amount of time—just the blink of an eye to her— but she'd belonged to him, heart and soul.

Hell, who was she trying to kid? She was using past tense, like she didn't love him or still belong to him, but the hard truth was, she did.

Did fate really have to give her such a strong blow?

Wasn't being cursed to begin with enough? Now she had to have *him* for a mate, the one person who could break said curse, and she was in love with him to boot—and he was the biggest dickhead she'd ever known.

The sound of someone swimming reached her, and she glanced over at the cave entrance, although she had little interest in who it was. It was a distraction, and that was all that mattered.

Her eyes widened in the next moment when she saw Ailani swim inside. Her mouth opened and closed but nothing came out as she watched the relief cross her friend's face.

"I've been looking everywhere for you, Payton. When did you start hanging out in my old cave?"

"Lani, what are you doing down here? You haven't been this far down since your curse was broken. And I started sleeping in here after you stayed on the surface."

Ailani swam over to her, her green eyes compassionate and a tad bit worried. Stopping in front of her, she took her hands and squeezed them gently. "I had to come see how you were doing."

Sighing as the look in her friend's eyes started making sense, she fought the pain as it tried to overwhelm her again. "You heard about the shit with Gabe then, huh? I'm feeling epically stupid and massively used, but other than that..."

"Oh Pay," she whispered, her eyes sad. "I wish you'd stuck around and listened to Gabe when he tried to explain. It could have spared you from hurting so much."

Spine stiffening, Payton flicked her tail in agitation as she looked at Ailani with disbelief. "You're taking his side?"

"I'm not taking sides," Lani replied swiftly as she shook her head. "I promise I'm not. He shouldn't have waited so long to tell you. He put both of you through hell and it was never necessary. But—"

"He *didn't* tell me. I felt the bond starting to form and then I saw my scale marking on his forearm. I don't think he ever had any intention of telling me. He just wanted to get laid and I was the unlucky woman who was convenient for his urges."

"Think about what you just said, Payton. How are you convenient for him to sleep with? You're only on the surface for roughly three days a month. If all he wanted was to get laid, there were far more convenient women he could have turned to who would have jumped at the chance."

She couldn't stop herself from visibly flinching and Ailani shook her head quickly.

"I didn't mean it like that. I only meant that he's a good-looking man. He could have found a willing partner easily enough, if all he wanted was a one-night stand. He clearly wanted more than that, though, or he never would have started anything with you."

"How do you know that?" she asked, hating how small her voice sounded. "Maybe it was the fact that I could only be on land for three days a month that appealed to him. Less chance of running into a woman he slept with if she's stuck in a lake ninety-nine percent of the time."

"For one, because he had to realize he'd run into you over the years since you're my best friend and he's Eric's brother. And two, because he told me and Eric that himself, not even forty-five minutes ago. He would have told it to you, too, but you ran off before he could explain why he didn't tell you he was your mate."

"I'm not sure there's anything he could say that would make that all right. He knew how much I hated being stuck here, and he knew it was my mate that would break the curse. We talked about how lonely I was, how I wanted a family even before our clan was cursed. I feel like a petulant child saying all this out loud, because it's not his responsibility to break the curse, mate or not, but I'm hurt that he didn't even feel like it was worth mentioning to me."

Ailani was quiet for a moment as she bit her lip, and then she shook her head. "You don't sound like a child—you sound exactly like what you are, which is a woman who's hurting. But think about this for a moment. You know how Gabe was not that long ago. He pretends like he doesn't give a shit what Julie did, but she hurt him badly, and he still has deep scars from that. And when Mackenzie died, he shut down. He barely had any interest in living—is it any wonder that he didn't want to jump into being someone's mate?"

She exhaled as she considered her friend's words. She hadn't thought of it in that light, but while it eased a small fraction of her pain, it didn't magically take it away.

"I don't blame him for not telling me right away. But when we started getting closer, he should have told me then. And he definitely should have told me before we slept together."

"I agree with you. He should have. But I still think you owe it to yourself to go talk to him about this. Get it all out in the open. Gabe's spent so long being emotionally inaccessible, barely speaking to people... Cut him just a little slack here and try to remember he's probably forgotten how to talk to people about his emotions, or hell, even just talk to people period.

"I'm not saying just blindly forgive him. But go back up to the surface before you're stuck down here for another month and at least talk enough to clear the air. If you still can't forgive him, come back to my house or go to the cabins. Don't cut yourself off from everyone. I don't want you to stay down here and get depressed like I was. You don't have a Payton to cheer you up and knock it out of you like I had."

"I'd thought about just staying down here for the next hundred years or so," she replied with a small, wry smile.

"Nope. You're not allowed. You told me once if I didn't go up to the surface, you'd drag me kicking and screaming. Same goes for you. Take some time down here if you need to. But then go up, talk to him, and come see me. If you don't, I'll eventually come down here and get you. And you really don't want to make me do that."

Payton could see she meant every word, and she already knew she was going to do as she was told. Ailani might be smaller than her, but she'd seen her in a temper, and it wasn't a pretty sight. She had no intention of being on the wrong end of that.

Leaning in, she hugged her tightly before pulling back with a genuine, albeit small, smile. "Thank you. And I promise I'll come up to the surface eventually. I won't wallow in my misery down here like I planned on."

"Good. I'm gonna give you some advice, though. And I'm sorry if I'm pushing it here, but I want you to be happy. When Gabe starts explaining, listen with an open mind, okay? Really consider what he's saying. If you find you can't move past it, well, that's one thing. But don't throw away your chance at happiness because you're too hurt to really hear what he's telling you. Believe it or not—and you probably don't right now because you feel like he deliberately deceived you—he's hurting, too. It was blazing from his eyes and I could hear it in every word he spoke. Give him a chance, okay? That's all I'm asking."

Ailani gave her one last smile and then swam back to the cave entrance, pausing for a moment as she looked back at her. "Oh and I had Tai and Brandy leave another set of clothes for you on the dock by our part of the lake. I'm gonna ask Gabe to leave the clothes you wore last night by the lake at his house. That way, you have options no matter where you go out first. And who knew my best friend had it in her to go streaking? I sure didn't."

Payton laughed softly at the wink Lani threw her before leaving, and then she wrapped her arms around herself, considering her words. Her friend had a point with a lot of that. Gabe had been so closed off, so lost in his head over his daughter's loss, that she never would have expected him to tell her they were mates back in the beginning.

Payton had a point, too, though. He should have said something after they got closer, or if he still couldn't bring himself to then, at least before they slept together.

Ailani said he was still hurting over what Julie did to him too. She'd never considered that before, but now that she was, she could see where it had been lurking in his eyes and in the twist of his lips when he talked about his ex.

Well, it wasn't that he was still hurting over it, exactly. She was positive he wasn't. But it *had* twisted and shaped his view of women, and she wasn't sure why she hadn't seen that before. Maybe that was why he hesitated so long to tell her—because he wanted to make sure she wasn't like his ex before he took things further with them. Until he was sure he wanted to be with her.

She still thought he could have made his mind up about that before they slept together. But she'd been out of the dating game for a thousand years. No doubt, things had changed a long time since then.

Groaning at the back and forth her thoughts were doing, she ran her hand through her hair and gripped it in her fist as she started swimming in agitation. She was going to have to talk to him, there was no doubting that.

And she should do it soon. No way could she handle her thoughts going in every direction like this for another month.

Mind made up, she swam out of the cave, moving swiftly and with purpose to the side of the lake where he lived. No need to put this off longer by getting out where she usually did, because then she'd need to find a ride to his house, since she didn't have his phone number memorized.

Reaching her destination, she popped her head out of the water cautiously. She wanted to get dressed before she saw him, because she was *not* having this conversation naked. If he hadn't left her clothes out, she'd wait until he had.

There was no sign of him, but her clothes were in a neat pile on the shore, along with a towel. She felt the magic brush down her spine as she left the water, and then she hurried to dry off and dress. He'd even left her shoes out there, which she was grateful for. Shoving her feet inside them, she inhaled deeply, trying to quell her nerves as she dried her hair with the towel.

There was a part of her that thought she could never forgive him for not telling her, but there was a bigger part that was already begging her to. He'd made her so happy for a split second of time, and she knew they could have so much more than that—if she could listen with an open mind and try to forgive him.

But as much as she wanted to, the pain still eating at her soul told her she didn't know if she could.

Taking in another deep breath, she balled the towel up in her hands and walked toward his house, her heart racing faster with every step she took. Just as she reached the back porch, the door opened, and they froze as they stared at each other in surprise.

"I was thinking about your hair and ran in to get this. Thought you might want it if you came by here."

She glanced at his hand as he held it up, a quick smile curling her lips when she saw the brush he was holding. "Yeah, thanks."

He handed it to her and shuffled his feet, looking as awkward and unsure of where to start as she was. Clearing his throat, he backed away from the door and held it open. "Come on in. Might as well be comfortable for this. Do you want anything to drink?"

Shaking her head quickly, she went inside, praying he didn't want to get himself a drink or make chitchat. She didn't think her heart could take waiting any longer. The pain was already tearing it to pieces, and her soul started aching the moment she set eyes on him.

Why the hell did she think talking to him was a good idea? Because it sure as shit felt like it wasn't, since the pain got stronger the moment she set eyes on him.

They went into the living room and she kept her eyes averted from his as she brushed out her hair. The less he knew of what she was feeling, the better. He'd already seen too much of her pain, and she didn't want him to know he had this much power over her.

Who was she kidding? He probably already did.

"I didn't want to admit it, but Julie did a number on me."

Her eyes flew up to his as she paused in the act of putting the brush down, and her fingers tightened painfully around it as she nodded for him to continue.

"I told myself that all women were like her, but really, I just didn't want to risk my heart again. I knew they weren't, but it was what I told myself to justify not taking another chance. By the time I felt healed from what she did and from being fooled so thoroughly, Mackenzie was sick. And when she died..." Pausing, he swallowed hard, and when he looked at her again, the pain in his brown eyes stole her breath. "I didn't know how to go on without her, Payton. I didn't *want* to go on without her.

"I shut down. At first, it was because I just couldn't deal with losing her. I was numb for the longest time, and I pulled away from everyone. When I started feeling again... well, I didn't *want* to. Logically, I know there was nothing I could do to save her, and that I did everything in my power to get her well. But I felt like since she couldn't enjoy life anymore, I didn't deserve to, either. Every time I laughed or smiled or enjoyed myself, it felt like a slap in her face, because she couldn't do those things anymore."

Payton sucked in a breath as he paused again, fighting the urge to tear up. His words were hitting her hard—she'd known he shut down, but she hadn't known he felt guilty for living, that he felt like he hadn't even deserved to smile.

"Gabe—"

He shook his head quickly, staring at his linked fingers. "Let me get this out. It's harder than I thought it would be. I haven't opened up like this in a very, very long time. I probably should have, but I was so focused on staying shut down... Anyway, when I met you, I already knew about the curse and how it could be broken. So, I knew from almost the very start that I was your mate. And even though I was drawn to you from the very beginning, I couldn't do anything about it. I still couldn't allow myself to feel anything good, because it felt like a betrayal to Kenzie.

"And I thought you deserved better than me," he said, raising his eyes to meet her gaze, the pain in his eyes like a knife to her chest. "I was a surly, grumpy dickhead, and you're so bubbly and optimistic. I thought I'd make you miserable, that we'd make *each other* miserable, so I resolved to never tell you. I felt guilty because I knew I could break your curse, but I thought there was another potential mate out there for you, and you'd find him soon enough."

Swallowing hard, she shook her head, trying to find her voice. "There isn't. There will only ever be you."

"I know that now," he replied, his voice hoarse and his dark eyes shadowed with regret. "Ailani told me earlier. I swear I didn't know that then, though."

"If Ailani and Eric never mentioned it to you when they told you about my clan, there was no way you could have known. I understand why you didn't tell me right away and I don't hold that part against you."

"Only the next part. It's okay. Don't look like that. I hold it against me, too. That night we took care of Ariel together... something shifted inside me. I saw you, and myself, in a different light. I think finally holding the baby had a little to do with it—that and talking to you about Mackenzie. It reminded me of my little girl and how much she would hate the man I turned into after she died. I think she knew how I'd be, because she spent her last days lecturing me and Eric to not mourn her forever, to let her go and live our lives.

"Eric had a much better time with honoring her wishes, although I know losing her hurt him damned near as much as it hurt me. We did the opposite—he thought to himself that Kenzie was watching over us, so he'd do all the things she couldn't do anymore, and he'd smile and enjoy himself to let her know he was having a good time for her. I took it in the other direction—not able to do anything without hating myself for living while she couldn't anymore. But that night, with you and Ariel... it reminded me of her and how disappointed she'd be in the man I'd become."

A few tears spilled down her cheeks and she wiped them away with shaky hands, trying to breathe through the pain in her chest. But this wasn't pain over how he'd hurt her—it was pain over how much *he* hurt.

"I didn't know Mackenzie, but I don't think she'd be disappointed in you, Gabe. From everything you've told me, she was wise beyond her years. I think she'd understand that pain and life get in the way of who we are sometimes, and that it takes time to get back to who we were before our lives were torn apart."

He smiled at her, and while it wasn't a full smile, it wasn't the grimace he used to give in its place. "Maybe you're right. She knew me better than anyone. She probably knew exactly how I'd react to losing her, and that's why she spent her last days lecturing me instead of enjoying herself."

His voice broke and he glanced away quickly—but not before she saw the sheen of tears in his eyes. Her cracked heart broke again, and she said to hell with her pain. His was by far worse, and it outweighed the pain she felt. She still needed answers, but not so much that she couldn't go give him what comfort she could.

And that was what she did, standing from her chair and making her way over to the couch. Sinking down beside him, she took his hand in hers and squeezed tightly, shedding more tears as he turned toward her and buried his face in her hair.

He needed this—and only after he'd gotten out some of the pain he'd kept bottled up for three years would she ask for her answers.

CHAPTER 16

GABE WASN'T SURE HOW LONG THEY SAT THERE, Payton holding onto him as he clutched her, fighting and losing a battle with his emotions. But by the time he eased away, he actually felt a little better, and he couldn't help wondering why he hadn't gotten some of that out sooner. Maybe if he had, he wouldn't have fucked up with Payton so thoroughly.

Then again... there probably wasn't a person alive who could have eased some of his pain other than her.

Inhaling deeply, he pulled back, reluctantly letting go of her hand. He desperately wanted to keep his hold on it, but he hadn't earned the right to.

Yet.

She looked at him, her sky-blue eyes still wet from her tears, as she smiled tentatively. "I don't want to ask if that made it better, because I know nothing will really do that. But I hope it eased some of your pain, at least a little."

"It did. And I can only hope that I can ease the pain I caused you. I don't know if I can, but I'll spend the rest of my life trying, if you just give me the chance."

"Tell me the rest."

It wasn't an agreement to let him try, but it wasn't a

refusal either, so he was going to take it and pray she could give it to him one day.

"Like I said earlier, it felt different after that night. I took off so fast because not only did I have a rough time talking about Kenzie, but I could feel how different we were, and it honestly spooked me. And then I came back the next day, partly because I wanted to apologize for how I left, and partly because I couldn't get you off my mind. I was still in denial about that, but once I kissed you when I was dropping you off, I had to admit it to myself.

"Even after that, I was still trying to tell myself I was too fucked up to be your mate. I can't count how many lectures I gave myself about it the following month. And yet, I still found myself Googling what day the next full moon cycle would start."

Pausing, he turned toward her as he took her hands in his again, gazing into her light blue eyes and willing her to believe him. "Payton... honestly, I knew when I showed up yesterday that I wanted to see where this could go between us. But please believe me when I say that I didn't intend to take you to my bed last night. I was going to tell you before things went that far between us. I asked if you wanted to come back here just because I wasn't ready for the night to end. It wasn't because I planned on sleeping with you—I just wanted for us to have more time to get to know each other.

"Last night... it just happened, and it was the most amazing, beautiful night. I knew then I had to tell you the truth and hope you didn't hate me for it. I swear to you, I planned on doing it this morning. But you woke up before me and figured it out before I could. I'm so sorry that I didn't stop what happened last night. I should have. I know that. I should have told you before we made love, and I'm sorrier than you know that I didn't. I never meant to hurt you, and it's gutting me that I did."

A few tears spilled down her cheeks and she inhaled shakily, her fingers tightening around his for a moment. "I thought you used me. That you used the connection mates have just to get me in bed."

Pain squeezed his heart in a vice grip, from her words and the tears on her face. Letting go of one of her hands, he wiped her tears away with shaky fingers as he shook his head. "Never. I would never do that. I might have been a total asshole, Payton, but even I wouldn't go that far, even in my darkest days."

"I believe you," she whispered, and he closed his eyes against the relief they brought to his soul. "I'm sorry I didn't give you a chance to explain earlier. When I felt the bond forming and then saw the mark on your arm, I immediately thought the worst. But I should have given you a chance to explain before I ran out of here."

Shaking his head, he brought her hand to his lips and pressed a kiss to her knuckles. "No. Don't apologize for that. Your reaction was completely justified and warranted. I fucked up, baby. Bad. You just did what any woman would have, when faced with those facts." Pausing he took their joined hands and pressed hers against his chest. "The bond… is that what I'm feeling here? Like a painful ball of energy?"

Her lips curled up as her eyes slowly dried of tears. "Yeah. I felt the bond and I suspected then, but I didn't know for sure until I saw the mark. The bond can start right away, but the mark shows up after having sex."

"I actually knew that part—Eric can be an over sharer sometimes," he replied with a wink, his heart warming when she laughed. "And if I'd been thinking about something other than the passion you inspire in me, I would have made sure to tell you before we made love."

"I can't deny how much that hurt, but don't keep beating yourself up for that. I get it. After our first kiss, I went into the lake determined to keep my distance from you. I thought we weren't mates and I knew it would end badly for one or both of us. But when I saw you again, I immediately forgot my promise to myself. And I could have put a stop to us last night—and when it was happening, I knew I should—but when you touched me, my resolve crumbled to dust and I completely forgot all the reasons we shouldn't. So I, more than anyone, know how you could have forgotten that you had something to tell me."

Gabe let his gaze rove over her beautiful face before searching her eyes, trying to find the right words. "I don't deserve you—"

"Oh no," she interrupted hastily, putting her fingers over his lips. "No more of that. You deserve to be happy, Gabe. You deserve it more than anyone I know. And if I'm the one who makes you happy, you're damned sure getting me."

Kissing her fingers, he reached up and took her hand in his, twining their fingers together. "You *do* make me happy, Payton. More than you know. I was just going to say that I don't deserve you or your forgiveness, but I'm a selfish bastard, so I'm keeping them."

"Oh. Well, in that case, tell me more."

He chuckled before letting it fade away, gazing intently into her eyes and hoping she could *feel* his next words. "I love you, Payton. More than I ever thought I could love anyone else. I never thought I'd fall in love again, and I sure as hell never thought it could happen this fast.

"It freaks me out a little, because you've so quickly

become as essential to me as the very air I breathe. But I know it happens quickly for your clan and their mates, and besides, it feels right. Righter than anything I've ever felt. I want to be your mate. I want to marry you one day. I want to fall asleep beside you every night and wake up next to you every morning for the rest of our lives. I want babies with you, I want it all. I want forever, sweetheart. Nothing less than that will do."

The ball in his chest burned brighter at his words, but he ignored it, watching as her eyes filled with tears again—but this time, he could handle the sight of them, because he knew they were happy tears. She inhaled shakily, so much love and happiness shining from her sky-blue eyes that he thought he could drown in them and die a happy man.

"I want that, too. Everything you said, I want. I love you, Gabe. I've waited a thousand years for you, and I've dreamed about you that entire time, but you're even more than I ever imagined you'd be. I want to marry you too, and I want to have your babies. I want forever with you, too."

The ball in his chest burned brighter, stealing his breath, and from the way she clutched his fingers tightly enough to break them, he knew she felt it, too. When the burn finally eased, he could still feel the energy there, it just didn't hurt anymore.

He glanced over at her, watching as she smiled happily at him, the sight stealing his breath again. "What just happened to the bond?"

"It locked into place, fully formed," she replied shakily, still smiling at him as love and happiness poured from her eyes. "We just broke the curse."

His breath caught as his soul lightened, feeling so much in that moment that he couldn't speak. He'd never thought he could even feel emotions again like a normal man, and now here he was, feeling so many, and feeling them so strongly.

He'd never felt so alive, so whole and complete. Life wasn't perfect, and he knew they'd still face challenges along the way. A corner of his heart would always feel Mackenzie's loss, and there would always be a Kenzie sized hole in his life. He wished with everything in him that she could have lived long enough to meet Payton.

And he had a lot of groveling and apologizing to do to his parents and his brother. Eric, especially. He'd put up with a lot from him over the years, and he'd been snapped at more times Gabe could count, all because he tried to get him to live again, to find if not happiness, then contentment.

Just like with Payton, he'd spend the rest of his life making it up to him.

But for the first time in years, he felt love, happiness, and hope. And it was all thanks to the gorgeous woman sitting next to him, gazing into his eyes and clutching his hands tightly, her love for him visible with every breath she took.

"Thank God it's broken," he whispered huskily, his emotions overwhelming him—and for once, he didn't try to fight them. "I would have taken three days a month with you if it was all I could have, but think about how much more amazing our life is going to be now that we can truly be together."

"I can see it already and it's beautiful."

"Eric gave me a piece of advice, and I think this is the perfect time to take it."

"What's that?" she replied, arching an eyebrow.

Without replying, he untangled one of their hands and reached for his phone on the coffee table. Waking it up, he pulled up the still open YouTube tab and pushed play, grinning as "Kiss the Girl" played in the otherwise quiet room.

Payton's looked at his phone and then her wide eyes met his a moment before she busted out laughing. He chuckled along with her, finding her light giggles too appealing to resist, and then she finally calmed, wiping her eyes before looking at him.

"I remember when Tai sung the chorus to Eric one night, before Eric knew what Ailani was. That was his advice to you?"

"Yep. And it would be rude of me not to take it, right?"

"Hell yes, it would," she murmured, a smile lingering on her lips as she wrapped her arms around his neck, sinking into him.

Gabe dropped his phone to the floor, pressing his lips to Payton's as he eased her back onto the couch, vowing that he was going to do as the song said and kiss the girl for the rest of his life.

COMING IN SEPTEMBER

Two new releases in the Mountain Mermaids: Sapphire Lake world!
By Moxie North and Elisa Leigh

And for more Mountain Mermaid books, go to:
https://www.mountainmermaids.net/

Ghost

Book five in the Blood & Bone Enforcers MC series

More Books by Grace

Rogue Enforcers Series

Colton: Rogue Beginnings

Mountain Mermaids: Sapphire Lake

Under the Sea

Blood & Bone Enforcers MC

Control

Thief

Iced

Shield

War Cats

Zane

Karis

Jameson

Vynn

Kian

Rocky River Fighters

Heart of a Fighter

Fighting for Keeps

Fight Song

Fighting to Win

Red Moon Shifters

Unexpected Mates

Temporary Mates

Forever Mates

Bear Claw Shifters

Starry Night Sky

One Sunny Day

Misty Autumn Morning

Grace has been writing all her life, but never imagined she'd ever let anyone read her work. *Her eyes only*, for years and years, even though being a published author had been her dream since she was in fourth grade. Then, she had a story in her head that wouldn't stop taking over her every waking moment, and characters who wouldn't shut up, demanding to have their story told. She decided when she sat down to write that this time, she was going to do it right and go all the way—and thus Starry Night Sky was born.

Publishing it and letting others into her head, heart, and soul, was one of the hardest, and most terrifying, things she's ever done, but it was incredibly worth it. She writes paranormal shifter romances because it's her favorite genre as a reader, but she's begun branching out into contemporary, publishing her first book, Finding Their One, book one in the Three Hearts Trilogy, under the pen name Khloe Thomas.

She's lived all over, but she calls Texas home at the moment. She has an adorable little boy, two dogs, and addictions to Gilmore Girls—watching it every night isn't a bad thing, is it?—coffee, and tattoos.

You can follow and reach her at the links above—she welcomes it!—or email her at gracebrennanauthor1@gmail.com.

Connect with Grace

Sign up for Grace's newsletter and be the first to learn about new releases and upcoming projects. No spam, just info on her books!
Grace Brennan Newsletter:
http://eepurl.com/dvH545

To stay up to date, you can also follow Grace on Facebook:
Grace Brennan's Shifter Haven (reader group)
https://www.facebook.com/
groups/gracebrennanshifterhaven/
Facebook Page
https://www.facebook.com/gracebrennanauthor

Other ways to follow Grace
Instagram: @gracebrennanauthor
BookBub: @GraceBrennan